To Wendy

The
Paper
Coast

All best,

Jefferson Navicky

SPUYTEN DUYVIL
New York City

Grateful acknowledgements for the following publications:

"The Air Around Her Objects" as a finalist for The Machigonne Fiction Contest, published in *The New Guard*

"Elstor" in *Smokelong Quarterly*

"The Vibrations of Her Lines: A Scent Memory" in *ITCH Magazine* & *Hobart*

"Perhaps the Sea" in *Summer Stock Journal*

"To and From the Auction" in *Wordriver*

"Dr. White" in *Six Minute Magazine*

"Battery Steele" as the winner of The Maine Community Foundation Essay Contest, published in *Maine Ties.*

"Out Past Matinicus" in *The Journal of Experimental Fiction*

"The Folk Songs of Washington Country" in *Opossum*

"Portrait of Etta" in *Interrobang!*

"The Journey of the Swim" in *The Catch: Writings from Downeast Maine*

"A Response to These Disappearances" in *Cordite Poetry Review: LAND*

"Teaching at Night" in *Serving House Journal*

"An Absence in the Mouth" in *Dispatches from the Poetry Wars*

Library of Congress Cataloging-in-Publication Data

Names: Navicky, Jefferson, author.
Title: The paper coast / Jefferson Navicky.
Description: New York City : Spuyten Duyvil, 2018.
Identifiers: LCCN 2017049416 | ISBN 9781947980099 (pbk.)
Subjects: LCSH: Maine--Fiction.
Classification: LCC PS3614.A9328 A6 2018 | DDC 813/.6--dc23
LC record available at https://lccn.loc.gov/2017049416

FOR SARAH

The Paper Coast

"Not another human soul in sight: not in the fields or in the farmyards. This is the perfect thing. We're walking, we're out travelling, and you're wearing your denim, colored russet."

—*Artifacts of Ice Age Maine*, Stephen Petroff

ELSTOR

I.

The light, today, this late afternoon before I set off, is a wonderful fabric that comes up periodically over the western tip. One must be prepared to inhabit it.

II.

Every October, I leave Point Lace, where I've lived alone for years, to visit my friend Kurt at his family camp in New Hampshire for a three-day retreat. He brings his woodworking and I bring my paints and a few canvases. We work all day, separated by the thin walls, taking time out for a swim or a walk or a smoke break.

We catch a fish and cook it for dinner with a few beers. At night, we sit on the side porch and I read bits from the odd collection of books Kurt's family has acquired at the camp over the years (*Portrait of an Artist as a Young Man, Guide to Terra del Fuego, Born to Kvetch*) and Kurt reads Proust.

He is almost finished with the second book, *In the Shadow of Young Girls in Flower* (Viking 2002). Kurt, for most of his life, was never much of a reader, but for reasons even he can't explain, he loves Proust. It's like sleeping with a quilt your grandmother made, he says. It took him two years to finish *Swann's Way* and it has taken him almost three with this volume. He doesn't even know how many volumes remain, though he knows there's at least one more.

Kurt chuckles to himself at a line he's just read. "This guy is good," he says, then a few moments later, after looking to see how much more of the book he has left, "I'm never going to finish this god damn thing."

I go to bed and think I hear the ocean in my ears, though I know it's only the pines.

III.

Kurt sent me a postcard. On the front was a kitsch photo of the Portland Headlight. On the back, he wrote, "Finished *Guermantes Way*. No need to continue."

At the beginning of that afternoon, three things existed: Kurt's postcard (representing Kurt himself); Proust (who existed only vaguely in my memory); and my body.

I've never grown old before, I tell myself over and over again. I have to do this because there's a part of me that is certain I have.

Without pause, the clock continued in some unfamiliar cadence that I felt to be haphazard, herky jerky, speeding up unexpectedly, adding extra beats like an irregular heart. But I knew this to be untrue.

I'd read Proust almost thirty-five years ago in my mid

thirties. I'd gotten through the first volume, thought it good, vowed to continue to the next volume, but never did. This does not seem uncommon. The experience for me was like driving my pick-up through dense autumnal fog late at night, listening to a voice, slow and melodious, on the radio. Even after I'd turned off the radio, the voice continued, inexplicably, though I wasn't surprised. I tried to listen to it but had to pay so much attention to the process of driving through the fogged night that the experience eventually became too tiring to continue. I have long since forgotten anything about the actual text and Kurt's postcard brought its scent to mind, but as soon as I identified the presence, it vanished.

IV.

I came inside after a walk before lunch. A Fedexed letter from Kurt's daughter, Rebecca, was wedged into the crack of my door. I opened it. Kurt had died the day before, of sudden liver failure, a rare condition doctors hadn't seen on his horizon. The funeral was tomorrow. "Would you be willing to say a few words at the service?"

In the Celestial Empire, when an elder died unexpectedly, there was a reckoning on the site where he left his last pile of clothes. If the positioning was favorable, the soul went to Paradise. If not, the soul became a ghost whose task was to usher the living to its own reckoning, and the reckonings of one thousand others. After a thousand reckonings, the ghost was released.

V.

My body has weathered so many aspersions, knowing they would come to an end. It has been an extremely capable vessel, shuttling me through many shells and facilitating the small but impossibly important pictures that sustain me.

Later tonight, I'll leave Point Lace, travel all night, and reach my destination by morning. I have no idea what I'll say.

The Air Around Her Objects

Robert, who had returned to the city the preceding night, had promised to take me to Winslow Park, and although I had not mentioned it to him, I hoped that we might have lunch there. Instead he invited me to have lunch in a village restaurant south of the city with his mistress, whom we were to afterwards accompany to a rehearsal. We were to pick her up before noon, after leaving Winslow, at her house on the outskirts of the city.

~

I exchanged a few words with Justine. We cut across the village. The houses were sordid. But beside the most dilapidated of them, the ones that looked as if they had been scorched by a shower of sulfur, a mysterious shape stood, making its days along the faded street, a resplendent angel stretching the dazzling protection of its widespread wings in blossom: a pear tree. Robert walked ahead with me a little way and began to speak.

"If on a winter's night, a traveler who left Bowdoinham at the end of a day, night following him and turning with the bends of the road, were to glimpse the black branching wings of such a tree spread out against the deadened screen of darkness, he might not know its majesty. But upon rising in the morning and looking to the east, its pleasing form would be laced upon the golden screen of sunrise. How could this not bolster a traveler otherwise beset with melancholy at the difficulty of human interactions, indeed simple humanness, how could it not brighten him? He would neither know whose tree it was, nor would he care; he would neither know when, even if, it bore fruit, nor its exact age or height. The tree would simply etch itself onto his happiness. He wouldn't want to know its mysterious shade, not yet at least. A beautiful pear tree in a village."

~

Justine was so clumsy with her hands when she ate that one received the impression that she must appear extremely awkward onstage. She recovered her dexterity, I imagined, only when she was making love with the touchingly intuitive foresight of women who are so in love with men's bodies that they immediately sense what will give most pleasure to those bodies so different from their own. Did she allow such pleasure for herself, for her own body? Love often moves across body boundaries, pleasure to touch a duplicate, back and forth, back and forth. But just as often, and perhaps more, the pleasure only extends to one body, one love to the other's exclusion like a passenger on a train bound for Boston who is unable to look at the beauty of the countryside passing the window. Justine dropped her butter knife, which thudded off the arm of her chair before clattering to the floor. She gave a little laugh as if she had expected it to happen. I reached down to pick it up. "It's a little curse of mine," she whispered as I handed it back to her and our hands brushed when I retracted and she took the knife.

I was told by old men whose memories went far back, and by young women who had heard it from these old men, that if women like Justine were socially exiled it was because of their extraordinary dissolute past, and when I objected that dissolute conduct was no obstacle to social success, they described her actions as something utterly in excess of anything to be met today. On the lips of those who told the tale, her misconduct became something so terrible I was hardly capable of imagining, something on a catastrophic scale belonging in the same category as public defecation or the defilement of a rose. And yet, when pushed to elaborate on the specifics of the offense, those taletellers demurred, saying it was too awful to retell. "Perhaps another time, young man, when I am not eating." Indeed this would prove to be challenging as the old man relating this particular story seemed to be perpetually caught in the moment of lifting liver pate or a deviled egg to his lips.

~

I couldn't stop seeing her as a shadow, my shadow. If

the shadow is the body's representation, the silhouette is a representation of that representation. A silhouette is a good hole into which we throw light and dark, virtue and sin, the self and its double, the body and the soul. It was absence that most concerned me now. What was the shape of the air around her objects? How did whiteness swoop in to tuck itself against her figure? It was easy to see her form but to visualize her negative space was much more difficult. What was it that her arm extended into? The entirely worn fabric of the air. I'd come to accept that I would not know her silhouetted darkness, for no one can know another's night; it was the shapes around her, her white recesses and how she dwelled in them, that I would like to inhabit. I would like to breathe that air, and to discover into what ocean the air descends. She had suddenly restored to my keeping the thoughts, the shadows, and the souvenirs that I had thought lost to me. I could not have felt it with any more confidence. I was alone, but wanted to be with her—this woman who I'd thought so clumsy at first, who I thought even dull, and of course who was already spoken for by Robert, the person with whom I shared my closest friendship. The urge for her came on like a glove into which I did not even remember slipping my fingers. Soft, sorrowful fingers already incapable of tracing any other body besides the one silhouetted in my mind.

Weary, resigned, with still several unquantifiable hours stretched in front of me, the grey day stitched away its pearly cloud line, and I was filled with the thought that I was to remain lacking close contact with her and with no more degree of acknowledgement between us than between two acquaintances who share a mutual friend. I had the urge to write her a letter containing the plentitude of her body and my desire to live in it like a bather walking towards the edge of a dock about to dive into deep water. Such a letter would be undeniable. It would be a letter full of distinct phrases coming together in better light, and full of music. Let Go Music, New Form Music, Roxy Music, not Happy Forget Me Music, but music that would roll her into me with a little burst of bass drum, a well placed riff, Devil Dive Music, Come Home Music, New School Music, Old World Music. All of it in a letter in which, at its end and before my slanted signature, I would ask her to accompany me to a show at the Aphodian next week where a brilliant band would play all of the music mentioned above and to which we would dance all night, smelling each other's sweat amidst the stale blanket of beer and body odor.

~

Certainly it is more reasonable to devote one's life to women than to postage stamps, teapots, or even oil paintings and sculpture. Yet the collector's aesthetics do not pass unnoticed: the thrill of fully disclosed, unmitigated material desire; fine contours and shapely curves. There is nothing like desire to obstruct any resemblance between what one says and what one has on one's mind. Time presses, and yet it seems as though we are trying to gain time by speaking about things that are utterly alien to the one thing that preoccupies us. Robert invited me once again for lunch with Justine, this time along the seashore, breaking waves, but it was no longer the seashore that captivated my eye. It was to my heart that she spoke in her deadly way. Robert blurred in the background. It is not possible, in such a dangerous guise, to regard the kindling of the miracle as a thing to be desired. As I placed a cherry tomato between my teeth like a cat holds a beloved fingertip, I held it there for a moment, imagining it her nipple, before popping it with a sharp tick of my tooth, flesh and juice spreading throughout the deep ends of my mouth.

~

"What really worries me is that if we go on like this I may have to kiss you."

"What a lucky misfortune that would be."

I did not respond at once to this invitation. Another person might have found it superfluous, for Justine's way of pronouncing her words was so carnal and so soft that her speech alone was like a kiss. A word from her lips was a favor, and her conversation covered you in kisses.

Robert was away at a training near the border and Justine had startled me with a visit in the early afternoon. Her hands had, a moment prior, been spread palms up in front of me. I had told her of her life line, her love line, her Mount of Venus, the bands of luck, how her hands curl when opened from a fist.

She moved closer and began speaking words I no longer registered, only their soft flutter against my pain body as if a flock of nameless mottled birds simultaneously took flight, battering me with their feathered wings. I could not remember a more euphoric discombobulation, a cascade of lips crossing my borders.

~

Her quiet circles. Her blossoming face. Her flushed valleys. Her dark surfaces. I spoke these locations to myself because I believed there was such a thing as knowledge through the lips. I told myself that I was to know the taste of this bodily rose, my mouth beginning to move toward the cheek I had envisioned, the exact field of plump tautness I'd expected. Her talented neck. Drifting over the expanses in between and coming up against the clear barrier of the breastbone. But before my lips lose themselves, the turn of her nose. We kiss, our noses as ill placed as extra appendages. I would love to follow hers as it sniffed along my crevices for faint perfumes. All possibilities, and a solid rotation of the body brings so many more, plump dimples up the spine, my lips crushed against cheeks and my eyes no longer see. Nothing except for the accelerating speed at which the experimental phenomenon of unknown origins—the body—continues to unfold, folds unfold and unfold. Into my own body I more fully take the taste I so desired, a shift in which I watch myself watching her body lying in the soft rumpled bed. I can no longer feel anything aside from the buzzing of my own body and from which I never want to rise— simply to stay in this slip until the horizon blurs into a meaningless ploy.

In between moments of constant thought, I walked. The Pine Loop, Marginal Way, out to the Head Light, along the cobblestones of the Old Port, down congested thoroughfares, up the Hill and down to the Eastern beach, a boat out to an island and along its perimeter, inside the pocked and pitted interiors, through the compliments received from others, the Crane Way, the Harraseekett Loop, beyond the usual ambit of the known walks, to the State Pier where I drank bubble tea, to Long Wharf where I conversed with colleagues, seldom the most direct route, past the morning newspapers shouting at me, the longshoremen and the shop windows. I was pained by signs of affection, but what hurt most to see was that there were unhappy people in almost every house I passed. I wanted, more than anything, to utter the words "I am no longer in love," but I couldn't. I imposed all that movement upon myself, and yet the feeling was still there, tucked away into some inaccessible corner, refusing to make any gesture of availability and also refusing to show any signs of abatement.

Certain women are incompatible without the double bed in which we find appeasement at their side, whereas others, to be caressed with a more secret intention, need leaves blown by the wind, the sound of water in the dark, things as ephemeral and evasive as they are. I walked among such leaves, the season's first to fall. So surprising to notice a few golden leaves scattered across one's path. The air too possessed an ending chill. At this moment of the year, it is, and has always been, impossible for me to feel optimistic; happy in isolated moments, yes, but not ever settled in the over-arching turning, like a man who has just begun his afternoon walk at sunset. I had convinced myself, and indeed now it was too late to believe otherwise, that I was in love with Justine, this temperamental girl, my best friend's lover, someone, I suspected, who would have no qualms about shattering my paradoxical hope at a moment's notice. Hope? Was it that? Lust? Did I simply want to destroy myself? Whatever it once was had now taken on the tinge of early autumn, one or two leaves littered on the ground beneath an otherwise lush canopy, and around the edges of leaf, of stem and of self, I felt a sharp intruding nip, the sensation of falling and a drop in temperature.

~

Then the sun disappeared and the mist became denser in the afternoon. Darkness fell early, and I dressed for the evening, but it was still too soon to leave the house; I decided to send a car for Justine. It felt like the only thing to do. I was reluctant to ride in the car myself, not wishing to force my company upon her during the journey, so instead I sent a note with the driver to ask whether I might come meet her. I watched the car pull away, and knew the outcome of the evening would not be positive for me, but I was resolved, like a doctor about to begin a futile surgery, to set the process in motion. About forty minutes later, the driver returned and handed me a note on pink paper, scrolled and tied with a black ribbon. I observed myself pull the ribbon's knot and unroll the note. It began "Dear A——" and continued in four swift sentences to proclaim that she no longer wished to see me in social or intimate settings. "This has never been a wise decision," like it was a casual investment in petty stock, "I'm sure you'll agree, one that need not be mentioned to Robert." She then said she was leaving that evening for New York and would be there for two months, working as an artist's assistant. "Please don't bother trying to contact me there. Fondly," like a knife, "Justine"

I re-rolled the note, tied on the black ribbon and gave the note back to the driver, asking him to dispose of it. I had no other choice than to go out into the night to walk.

~

It was surprisingly restful to listen to Justine's speech floating across and through the mild cacophony of voices in the reception hall. Her voice possessed the eerily perspicacious quality that could find me within the densest wall of sound. Expressing some slight thing of the moment, it was singularly pointed, as if I was alone in her company and she condescended and clarified the melody of her speech to the point of an old song on the record player, a warbling soprano, the crackling of the arm's needle and dust. Then, as I risked a sidelong glance at Justine, I could see, calmly imprisoned in the unending afternoon of her eyes, an expanse of sky above an island in the bay, bluish, thin and slanted at the same angle of incline as Robert's eyes. Indeed she was speaking of him, one of his recent accomplishments, in the breathless, idiot manner of touching idolatry, a blanketing love as evident as gravity. I could never tune out her voice. Exiting through the kitchen, walking between waiters and the smell of seared meat, I left the crowded air, knowing that I would not return.

Journey to the Timor Islands

A light snow was falling as Charlie Reardon left the diner and made his way down Madison Street. He didn't want to be the kind of person who 'made his way' anywhere; he wanted to confidently 'stride' or boldly 'strike out' towards Madison, but he had to admit to himself that this was not the case. One could've even substituted the verb 'trudged' or even 'shuffled' into the sentence and Charlie would've only raised an eyebrow at the descriptive truth.

The truth, Charlie Reardon thought, is a very strange thing. He forced himself to fall back upon the unsatisfying conclusion that while there are, beyond doubt, certain combinations of occurrences and reasons which make up a truth, the analysis of its amorphous soul lies among considerations far beyond his ken.

Charlie's toothpick prodded sesame seeds left over from his dinner. The wind against his neck did not feel good, and yet he continued in the direction of the ocean, the direction from which the wind poured. Such thinking, he unavoidably thought, did not lead to any kind of happiness; truths are best left unexamined and instead accepted as what they are: unknowable masses that just feel right.

When Charlie Reardon reached the end of Madison, before he crossed into the crosshatch of streets along the wharves, he could see the Winslow's immensity making vertical strikes into the quickly darkening sky. The snow increased in severity and Charlie knew that the gray belt out in the bay would make their departure tonight difficult.

Charlie trudged, he freely admitted it now, towards the Winslow, his eyes slowly rolling themselves open, looking for the signs of the troubling truth he knew he would discover. As he got closer to the Winslow, Charlie saw Ms. Hazzard, her thick bulk clad in her customary black wool cape, standing on the fore deck. White flakes caught on the coarse weave and Charlie thought she resembled a mountain.

Reardon! Ms. Hazzard called out and despite the muffling snow, Charlie clearly heard her. We sail in a half hour, she said and with that Ms. Hazzard vanished from deck. Charlie now knew what was expected of him, knew that if he could ever turn and run as fast and as far away from the Winslow, now would be the time. Simultaneously he knew that he would never turn away to run. He'd never get away, and further more he didn't even want to; the truth would follow him no matter where he went. Charlie burped up the faint smell of french fries and even though it was a little disgusting to him, he also savored it as a further reminder of what would most likely be his last proper meal as a Stoker.

As Charlie descended the stairs to the boiler room, Ms. Holiday stopped him, firmly but quietly grabbing him by the elbow. Without looking into his face, she said, we will need all the power you can generate.

Ms. Holiday said this almost breathlessly. Where are we sailing to, Ms. Holiday? Charlie asked. The Timor Islands, she responded and left without another word. These were more words than Charlie had ever spoken with Ms. Holiday or anyone on the Winslow, and in fact in his many years of service aboard the ship, he'd often wondered if Ms. Holiday, and indeed every woman aboard the Winslow, for he was the only man among the crew, was mute, or at least if they'd simply chosen never to deign conversation upon a lowly Stoker.

Charlie took off the wall the large iron shovel he'd so often lifted, striding, finally striding, toward the coal bin. The fire from the furnace immediately caused him to break out in a sweat and the movements of his arms, the dig and pull, the squat of his legs, all felt so good to him, so familiar like he was finally home. The ship rolled and plunged in the rising storm and with each pitch of the hull beneath him, Charlie felt the truth all the more solidly in his body and continued, harder, to dig his shovel into the sooted mass, throwing the fuel into the fire. The rhythm made his body sing, and he realized he'd never been happier. The Timor Islands? Charlie Reardon had barely heard of them—they were so far way—but he knew he would not live to see the port. Would they find another Stoker? He was sure they would, but such things were not his problem. He felt sure about this, as sure as there is a sea where the ship itself will grow in bulk like the living body of the seaman. Charlie turned once again, as he'd done so many times before, away from the pulsing furnace and dug his shovel into another load of coal.

To and From the Auction

It was still Sunday morning dark when I poured the coffee into the thermos and we started to drive north. Between sips, I ate a coffee brandy doughnut as I drove. Deanna dozed in the passenger seat as the sky lightened. Dawn officially opened somewhere around Brightonville, at first a pink sting swelling and then a blossoming of night's bow. After almost two and a half hours, we parked along the edge of the road, our car tilting off toward the ditch. We walked past a row of cars, mostly trucks, parked along both sides. Deanna kicked some stray pieces of gravel from the shoulder into the bushes. I'm tired, she said, but I could tell she wasn't all that tired. Wait 'til we get us some egg saniches, I said. Nothing better than a buck-fifty egg sanich. I could tell Deanna was ready for the auction by the way she said, "sanich", like she was already taking a bite of the grilled English muffin and the crispy bacon edges of the egg.

Even though it was only 7:35, the lower barn was already packed with people, its cement floor an unforgiving place to spend the next four hours, but it would be worth it, I hoped. I didn't know exactly what I wanted to bid on, even after I'd scrolled through the grainy pictures of the lots on the website, but there was some strong feeling propelling me to attend. I'd attended a few other times before, but had never bought anything.

Actually I'd never even bid on anything because the entire haphazard melee of the bidding intimidated me. Half the time I couldn't even understand what the head-setted man sitting in the auctioneer's seat was saying, let alone bolster myself for a bid, my timid hand inching up in a two-fingered flag. But oh, did I dream of bidding, a confident stream of wags and ticks and flicks and nods, all acknowledged immediately and effortlessly by the auctioneer.

Deanna, during the drive, had actually asked me, so you're going to bid on something this time, really? I gripped the steering wheel harder, glaring at the road. Of course, I said, wanting it to sound off-handedly confident. Come on, really? Deanna had woken up a little more at the sight of my insecurity. It's nothing to be ashamed of, she said, if you might be a little intimidated to bid at that auction—it's a crazy place. I couldn't admit this fear to Deanna, as we'd only begun dating a few months ago and I still held to my projection of bold manliness in her eyes, though I'm sure she saw right through me on date one. But still, I had my pride. Deanna was the kind of person who wouldn't blink at bidding, and indeed winning, exactly what she wanted. In fact, she'd bought herself a lawn mower at the auction a few weeks ago, a real prince of a machine for fifteen dollars. She cut her lawn last week and it looked great, like a smooth cut skull. The early morning auction had been my idea of a date, but so far, it was Deanna who distinguished herself in the art of acquisition. That would change today.

I milled about through the lots in the barn. The bidding had not yet started, but would soon. I had a few precious moments to get my bearings, find out what was calling me today. Thankfully, Deanna was occupied at another side of the barn, mulling through one of the furniture lots. I shuffled by a box of old farm tools, a beautiful Remington typewriter, a scarecrow wire skeleton—so many tempting things, but none of them called to me.

Then I stubbed my foot on a box of books on the floor. My first instinct was an expletive, as the stubbing really hurt, and my second instinct was to hurl the box of books across the barn in a fit of rage. But I restrained myself on my second urge, and instead I bent down to examine the contents. James Paterson, *The Grapes of Wrath*, *The Prophet*, Clive Clussler. Ho hum. Nothing to see here. I dug a little deeper and to my surprise I unearthed a beautiful cloth-bound edition of Shirley Hazzard's *Glass Houses*. I'd read all her other books and thought she wrote perhaps the most beautiful sentences in the English language. *Glass Houses* was the only book of hers I hadn't read and in fact, I didn't even know it existed. How had this little book escaped my awareness? I had no idea, but now I knew of it. And my pounding heart told me I really wanted to own it.

Three hours later, my limbs shaking from nerves, I carried the box of books—Lot 410—to the car as its new owner. Of course I had built up the bidding process well beyond reality. Though visibly sweating, I managed to shoot up an arm and five second later, as I was the only bidder, I owned the box of "some mystery books," as the auctioneer called them, for $3.75. It was all alarmingly easy and I felt quite smug. The bidding was still in full swing, and in fact wouldn't probably stop for another several hours (they still had to get through the Upper Barn). I heard the auctioneer's gravelly voice barking in the back of my head, but it was a few moments before the fact registered that Deanna was locked in a bidding war over a barrister's bookcase, a real beauty of a piece, mahogany, each shelf with its own sliding glass door. The bids flew up like popcorn. I gasped. And then held my breath. Suddenly Deanna raised her hand and the auctioneer indicated that she had bought the barrister's bookcase. For how much? I didn't want to know.

On our drive south, my car weighed down to a dangerous sag with the bookshelf strapped to the roof, Deanna said she'd bought it so there could be a place to put my newly-bought books. Deanna worked at the fish market along the wharves, didn't make all that much money, and thus a bookcase was a significant purchase for her. We don't even live together, I said, a little befuddled. Well, she said, slowly drawing out a questioning smile, maybe we should.

~

The apartment we rented together smelled faintly of bitters mixed with sawdust, not an unpleasant smell by any means, but certainly a distinctive one. We'd lucked into a deal of an apartment on the Hill, a turn of the century, high ceiling, intricate molding one-bedroom with a huge double parlor. However, between Deanna and me, we had hardly any furniture, our bed a mattress on the floor, no couch but one mostly uncomfortable armchair; we ate our meals on the foldout coffee table trays that had been my grandmother's. We lived mostly in the middle of all our too many rooms because we'd piled and stacked our miscellany along the walls (no closets). The effect gave the apartment a fox den-like feel, like we were walking through tunnels to get from the kitchen to the dining room to the last room of the double parlor. Deanna called it our fallout shelter. I thought we were just waiting for one of us to appear on one of those game shows where, through some stroke of dumb luck that masks itself as skill or knowledge, we win a dining room furniture set or a living room furniture set or even a bedroom set. Of course I doubted we would actually like any furniture we'd win on a game show—too much like the showroom of a Lazy Boy factory or someplace like that—but we could sell all that stuff and go back to the auction and buy our real soul furniture.

The sole exception to our barren apartment was the

barrister's bookcase that we'd placed in a spot of honor in the front parlors against the chimney where it could be easily seen. It was filled with the books I'd bought as Lot 410 and even though we had other piles of books scattered throughout the apartment, we decided that the contents of this bookcase would only ever be the books of Lot 410. We'd build the rest around it.

One day, not so long after we'd first moved in, I took the Shirley Hazzard book from the bookcase. I still hadn't read it and was in fact a little scared to read it, as if reading it might break some kind of spell that the book had fortuitously placed on us. So in lieu of reading the book, I simply thumbed through it. As I did so, a piece of paper fluttered out to the floor, a square scrap of something handwritten on one side. I picked it up. It was a hand-drawn map of some sort. Upon examining it further, I noticed it was a map of our neighborhood on the Hill, and indeed an "X" sat where our apartment stood. The rest of the map detailed, to my surprise, a route north to the auction where I'd bought the book. I didn't recognize the handwriting and if it was Deanna's, then she'd learned a way to write in a completely foreign script than her normally delicate curve. But I doubted this very much because the script was blunt and forceful, the markings having been made by some thick tip. Every turn on the map was accompanied by little notations—"Johnson's Quarry" and "River Run Road"—even small roads whose names escaped us were all there in this rough scrawled detail. The map had no title or name on it or otherwise identifying marks, just the pure black lines. The most alarming aspect of the map was that, no matter how hard I tried to decipher the fact, I couldn't tell if the map led from our apartment to the auction or vice versa. After a while, this puzzled me so much that I could feel a vague but mounting panic start to rise within me. Deanna walked by, holding a cup of coffee. What's wrong, she asked, taking a sip from her mug. Oh, nothing, I said, quickly stuffing the piece of paper back within the book and placing it back on the shelf. Nothing at all. Probably nothing whatsoever to worry about.

THE BOLERO

The roads were dark on our way down. The marina glittered a slick black sky on water. Slight wind brought a chorus of clickings, metal against masts, and the gently insistent slap of moorings. I felt a chill as soon as we were on the water, and I wished I'd brought another layer. The Composer, in his usual tweed, now looked prescient, whereas in the starkness of a summer day, his tweed looked too tweedy, not to mention too hot. The Bolero dwarfed all other boats anchored in the small marina. Her windows glowed a subdued orange.

As soon as we saw her moored out there, my breath shortened and the nerves began to hum. Down the ramp, we made for her. I began my usual panic countdown. Should I say something? When? As usual, I gave in immediately: "Should we be doing this? We don't have to—" The Composer held up his hand in a musical gesture. "We need to do this," he said. "You need to do this."

The Composer knocked quietly on the door to the Bolero. A woman in black opened the door. She recognized the Composer. "He's with me," the Composer said. "It's alright." The woman in black shrugged: "Fine. But he can't play." We both nodded. I felt a surge of pride I would soon regret.

Life on a yacht is a lot of narrow hallways and small

rooms. No matter how many times I accompanied the Composer on his jobs, I was always surprised by such particulars. This effect was magnified when the lady in black led us to a room that, when we entered it, seemed to be filled solely by the presence of one finely-dressed, rotund woman. She spread.

"Madam Nut," the Composer said and bowed deep.

I felt the distinctly uneasy sensation of entering a denizen world whose customs and motivations were unknown to me, hidden perhaps for my own good or perhaps through an ignorance all my own. I was never especially astute in such foreign situations. Whatever the reason, and I wished I didn't do this, I began to feel suspicious.

We squeezed in beside Madam Nut.

"Welcome to the Bolero." Madam Nut spoke in a low voice that sounded like an excavator through gravel.

The rest happened very fast.

"How was your summer?"

"Excellent. Fresh start?"

"Oh yes. Too short."

"Too short! Always."

"Fish?"

"Yes."

"Accompanied?"

"Yes."

"Sauce?"

"Yum."

"Loafers?"

"Penny."

"No."

"Why?"

"Too much."

"Oxfords?"

"Fine."

"Whatever."

"Beef isn't possible anymore."

"No! Gas?"

"Gone."

"You park like an asshole."

Madam Nut laughed a belly laugh like a dump truck backfire. "You are a funny guy, Dennis. You're weird. I like you. Now play for your keep."

That's when I heard the first explosion. Somewhere out in the marina. "Holy shit!" I exclaimed and thwacked my hands down on the table top. "What was that?" Madam Nut laughed again, this time like a steamroller. The Composer smiled shyly.

"That sounds promising," Madam Nut said. "Should we stay here or proceed to the deck?"

"That depends on if you want to die or not," the Composer answered.

"What do you recommend, life or death?"

"Again, that depends."

I thought of my kid and my wife. I wanted out. The second explosion, much nearer, rocked the Bolero and I pitched forward, ramming my rib cage into the table edge. The door to the room flew open and the lady in black rushed in.

"The marina is on fire. We must leave immediately! The police are on their way."

"What have you done, you fool?!" Madam Nut reached across the table to grab the Composer. "You've gone too far!"

"Sometimes the music is chaos, Madam Nut," the Composer said.

That was the Composer's final performance, his last composition, his last words, the culmination of his creative acts. Or it wasn't. Not on purpose. I don't know, maybe he just screwed up and accidentally blew himself up in the process, along with everyone else on the Bolero. Except me. I don't know how I made it out. It all happened so fast. I was lucky. I was cursed. I'm the elegy. I'm the coda. I hear the music in my head. But I don't know how to get it out. I'm lost without him. The world is a cruel container. It used to be much easier. I'd like to say that I'll find another partner and my collaborations will continue, but instead it seems like the explosions started with him, and they just keep coming.

KITES

My fiancé and I travel north. We stop into a little coastal town known for its ice cream and lobsters, and wander into a fabric store tucked away down an alley. As we stand behind a turquoise-tiled countertop, a small, wiry gray-haired woman emerges from a backroom. Without even a glance in our direction, she launches into a torrent of complaints and obscenities as she paces back and forth. Behind the counter, hundreds of handkerchief-sized piles of fabric await, spread like crumbs, each a different color. As the woman rants, she walks around gathering individual pieces of fabric from the sea of colors. She has amassed a significant pile before I realize that, without a word from either of us, she has been culling all of my fiancé's favorite colors, all the colors that somehow hue her personality. As we watch the woman work, my fiancé and I quietly hold hands as if we are standing along the sidewalk while the slow parade of her soul ambles by.

FISCHER'S RETURN

The phone rang.

It was as if I had asked for something without knowing it, and then suddenly my wish was granted. This startled me, for I had to face the reality of receiving exactly what I wanted, not a concession or a partial accumulation with strings attached, but the exact thing: to stay on the island for an extended period of time with good work to do. Once I'd secured the house from the aging father of a college friend who no longer ventured out of Manhattan, thus providing me with virtually unlimited accommodations, an indefinite stay became easy. Island work on the other hand was nearly impossible to find, and that was an understatement. For a few months at the beginning of my stay, I'd worked as an assistant to a part-time carpenter who taught art as an adjunct at a college on the mainland. As it may sound to those familiar with this kind of intermittent work, actual employment was rare and Bill could only afford to pay me, on average, $100 for a job that usually lasted twelve to fifteen hours, spread over a sporadic period of days according to his grading and teaching load. It was hard manual labor and I was the thirty-nine year old grunt, hauling wheel barrels of rubble, climbing ladders with thirty pounds of shingles balanced on my shoulders, work with which my seventeen year old body would've struggled and which was a far cry from the cushy literary archival work I'd performed in New York where I'd been surrounded by yellowed and curling typewritten pages, must, dust, and handwritten notes from the early part of the twentieth century. I sifted dirt; the turned loam replaced the beautiful stale page, the nail stronger than the pencil. My starting-to-flab body suffered for a while, but I soon grew to love the toil and the strain, the way my body looked forward to its growth and appetite, how my mind sharpened itself on the work's stone, a harder sweat, crisper mental air, quieter, and especially the satisfaction at the day's end, sharing sandwiches and beer with Bill.

But now that would be over, or at least I would only help Bill when I could, when both our schedules met. The first installment of the advance would arrive in two weeks and I would begin my translation, a different type of shoveling, loading my wheel barrel with Fischer's words and carrying them across the river. As I worked, Fischer talked to me, retold me his story, its subtleties as I gleaned them from his innuendos, and I asked him questions, asked him to repeat, slow down, a type of interview with the departed for which the only transcription was the book, his book, then mine, but for the veracity of the latter, of course, one can only take my word.

In the cabin on Peaks, there was a canary yellow rotary phone with a seven-foot cord mounted to the kitchen wall. I gave out my number only to Beatrice and a few others, but as I stood in the kitchen reading the letter, I had the thought to forgo my usual postal response. Alex Gallo had a 212 number, plus an extension, embossed in blue and gold across the letterhead. As soon as I'd dialed the number, I regretted the decision. A corporate voice with a headset answered and I immediately hung up in fear. In the letter to Gallo from my kitchen table, I wrote, Dear Alex, I've just read your letter, and though I wonder how you found me (even the island post office isn't sure I exist and they know everyone's address), I am more than willing to do the translation of Henri Fischer's *Hubbard's Return*. It's a book I've always admired from afar [this was partially a lie]. I'm in a perfect setting to do such work and will begin immediately. The old man could write a hell of a sentence, and it's an incredible book. You've made a wise decision to include it in your series. I'm honored and grateful to work on it. Sincerely,

I probably wrote some other things, hurriedly vague sentences meant to fill a little space on the page while not saying anything stupid that could cause Gallo to retract his offer. I addressed the envelope and was struggling about whether to lick the flap or find some other means of moisture when I realized the phone was still ringing and had been doing so for some time, a pleasant thrumming, mechanical in a way that one could feel its inner mechanisms beckoning. I had no answering service and often enjoyed letting the phone ring for a very long time. Beatrice began speaking to me before I said hello, breathlessly relaying a recipe for Russian teacakes that she had recently attempted. Somewhere in her stream of words was an invitation for tea that afternoon, or rather, I realized, she invited herself to my cabin for tea. Then it will be a celebration, I said, because I've found a way to stay on the island.

When the book was originally published, a friend called it one of the strangest autobiographies ever written. I sometimes called it the longest autobiography ever written, all three hundred sixty pages of it, although I did tend to agree with my friend's opinion. Regardless, after many years, I still hadn't read the entire cursed thing when the letter from Ultima arrived. An editor, a man named Alex Gallo, said he had heard I would be a strong candidate to perform the new translation. There had been one dubiously subjective translation in the seventies, but nothing since. Alex insisted on remaining ambiguous as to who had recommended me for the task and this might normally have been disconcerting, but since I had been living in a rented house on a island in the northern Atlantic for almost a year, only making occasional pilgrimages to the mainland for a matinee or a lecture and quickly running out of savings, I figured whoever had heard of me was either taking pity on my isolation or was relying on some past accomplishments, which were startling slight and generally lacking in my mind. Either way, the intrigue of the job was too great to turn down. I was undeniably content, in my own ascetic way, living in the interior of the island, with regular ventures to the beaches, sometimes with Beatrice, but the prospect of Fischer's prolonged company was a very attractive bridge.

I tried to put myself on a schedule. My lofty goal started at three translated pages a day, a reasonable goal, I thought, even if it would be challenging. Some days would be easier than others, and I would take breaks, lots of breaks. I'd get into good shape, get into a good rhythm and it would all go quicker. It's fine to not make the goal every day, just most days—these were the things I told myself to bolster my confidence and momentum at the project's start. I think I made my three pages probably twice in the first week, and hoped this number would rise as the weeks progressed, but it didn't happen that way. I translated three pages in a day only one time after that initial week, weeks and weeks of piddle. At this pathetic rate, it would take something like ten years before I finished. Most days I struggled in a blindness whose affliction I couldn't name, let alone understand. What was wrong? I knew all the words in French; I enjoyed the linguistic tinkerings, the synonym bopping; all I had to do was establish Fischer's syntax and move forward. It really shouldn't have been so hard. But I could not concentrate. It was like a fog fell on not only the entire island, but epicentered on my head every time I sat down to work, a kind of flip-the-switch fog that lifted immediately as soon as I gave up for the day. And oh did I ever begin to give up easily.

I sure wanted the next installment of my advance, but I was very unlikely to get it. Beatrice would stop by with a picnic basket of custard pie and beer—want to have a picnic at the ball field? Pie and beer, you want to have picnic of pie and beer, I asked. Doesn't that seem like a strange combination to you, and don't you know I have to work? I thought you might want a break, she said. Pie and beer, that combination is a little gross—that's what's supposed to tempt me, seriously? It's a homemade custard pie? And it's really good beer. Beatrice kicked up one heel. She put on a very good perky when she wanted to. Admittedly it didn't take very much to convince me. You're a push over, Beatrice said, for a guy who's supposed to be a professional translator, you don't do a very good job being a pro.

I began to think myself hopeless. Once I'd been a capable translator of French, so capable in fact Mr. Alex Gallo, who probably had a carpeted shwag of an office somewhere in the Ultima suite on some 15th floor in midtown, had heard of me and thought me good enough. That was sure a mistake.

Then I got a request for an interview about the project from *The Dedalus Forum*, a literary magazine whose timing couldn't have been worse.

The Dedalus Forum
May 2006

In 1964, the twenty-year-old Henri Fischer traveled to Labrador to follow the journey of cartographer

Leonitus Hubbard who, one hundred and three years ago, starved to death in that wilderness. Fischer wrote his enigmatic travel work a year later in the fallout of the experience. The book, written in French, earned a cult following for its savage intensity. Roberto Auden has begun a new translation of Fischer's book, estimated to appear in print late Spring 2007 from Ultima Press.

DF: Mr. Auden, Fischer's book is known more as an experience of suffering than a piece of travel writing. Can you speak about how this comes through in the current translation?

RA: *Hubbard's Return* is a travel book in the sense that Fischer traveled to Labrador and wrote a book about his travels, but at that point, it departs. Before the book begins, before the reader witnesses his fate, the narrator's course of action has been fixed. Beside the title's allusion to Leonidus Hubbard's ill-fated 1903 journey, Fischer makes no other references to him, and does not make any effort to vindicate or eulogize Hubbard. There is no introduction, no scene setting, and no reasons for the story. All these are brushed away with the candor of the opening sentence: "I traveled to Labrador to open a void." That is the metaphysical extent Fischer allows himself. The rest of the book faithfully records the vagaries of Fischer's mind, allowing each thought until it dissipates. The work is devoid of plot, action, and other than the narrator, character. In many ways, the writing could take place anywhere, with the substitution of Labrador for any other site, urban or rural, lonely Bowery apartment or bus in an Alaskan wilderness, because, other than serving as the completely passive backdrop, the landscape has no effect on Fischer. He ignores it, resents its presence, but tolerates it as he does all other things (tent, hiking boots, bag of rice) he relies upon for survival. He suffers in the extreme, either from starvation or dysentery or cold, but he makes it clear that he chooses to suffer. There are some vague allusions to anger towards his father, but it becomes clear that he has chosen to do this because he wants to, he feels he needs to, beyond reactions against patriarchy or capitalism or any other of the twentieth century's mendacities. Pity doesn't exist. Fischer's actions are a form of athleticism by which he pushes himself to the brink of death and stays there as long as possible, in a type of perfect solitude, allowing all other concerns to drift away. He says at one point, "After a while, when I hadn't eaten in a long enough time, my brain simply ran quiet and my head floated in light." Identity disappears. Nothing inhabits his mind, but eventually the question: live or die? There is no redemption, no salvation. Live or die, which one? Does the soul choose to devour itself or can it retract such cannibalism? He reaches the last strand between self and world. Does he choose to break it? At the end of the book, Fischer chooses to live. He walks out of the wilderness. Is this a success or a failure? He ends the book there. It's that clear sense, the thin air of such an elevation, that I try to portray in the translation.

DF: The story itself shares quite a few parallels with Knut Hamsen's *Hunger.* Do you address the similarities?

RA: Not really. Literature is full of borrowing and flat out theft. Rather than get all caught up in the fine points of possession, I tend to think of these loose exchanges as fodder, or compost, for new, great works of literature. With that said, *Hunger* must have been an influence on Fischer, however the differences are significant. For one, Hamsen's protagonist suffers in a dense city—Fischer struggles through the Labrador wilderness, a place much more vitally wild and potentially dangerous. In Hamsen's book, one has the feeling that the flourishing world is within reach if only the narrator can tap into it; this is not the case with Fischer's book. The Labrador wilderness is not a forgiving place. Fischer also encounters no human soul. That's part of the true wonder of the book in that he creates this present-moment chaos travelogue solely through his own actions. And while a reader might wonder if this would get boring after the first one hundred pages, the alarming truth is that it doesn't. The book is journalistic, a type of log, but his prose has an electric quality like it's bouncing off the foundation of a traditional sentence. Fischer claimed it, and the book was published as, travel writing, a pioneer of such hybrid works. Hamsen's *Hunger* is a novel, though usually thought to be based in personal experience; Fischer makes a bolder claim of fact. Can the accuracy of his story be checked? Of course not, but Fischer makes it feel true. A reader easily trusts him and his madness; that is his greatest accomplishment as a writer of this strange book.

DF: And why the need for the new translation?

RA: Because the publisher asked me. The 1971 translation is rough, like a bone was broken and set quickly. It conveys Fischer's muscular prose, but, as I hear it, there is a subtle poetics to *Hubbard's Return* and I want to apply heat and skill to achieve a finer edge.

That interview made me feel like a dirty phony. I talked so authoritatively, or so I hoped, about this book on which I purported to be an expert. But in reality, I was nothing near it—I was a complete failure, a ribboning mess of insecurity and distraction. It was no surprise that immediately following this heinous interview, my ability to translate Fischer's book completely and utterly left. I couldn't even bring myself to translate a sentence, even one word struck me with a revulsion so deep that I felt physically ill. Beatrice thought it allergies. I didn't contradict her, though I also didn't tell her of the grinding halt of my work. After a few days of dejection stretched out into a week and threatened more, Beatrice thought I had a viral infection and was dedicated to the act of ministering to me, bringing me chicken soup even though it was now the onset of warm weather, temperatures rising toward the 80's, and the thought of hot chicken soup boiled my soul. Yet Beatrice continued, moving to cold compresses when I protested with a sweating forehead. But most of the time I was left alone to suffer my own prideful fallacies, spending the majority of my day prone in bed, staring at a boring ceiling during the time I'd previously dedicated to work. I literally and physically atrophied and it will probably come as no surprise that soon I doubted if I would even be able to work ever again. I envisioned Alex Gallo's letter rebuking my galling lack of productivity, claiming that he'd expected so much more, something about a "profound disappointment." Of course, in my hallucinatory day dreams, I declined or forgot or was unable to answer his letter, causing a more pressing, exclamatory letter to arrive, in which I was called things like: chicken! hypocrite! loser! Idiot! Asshole and Fool! This all felt good in the way a hairshirt must feel to an unrepentant sinner.

Still, nothing changed, at least no everyday realities altered. The Dedalus Interview was published. Alex Gallo sent me, not a remonstrative note about my productivity, but a congratulatory one, saying he thought the interview helped to generate the book's "pre-publication buzz." This made me sick. My family and friends, those who read such things as *The Dedalus Forum* or heard about it, congratulated me on my work, you are so impressive, we always knew, good for you... my baby boy, etc. Soon I thought I would never rise from bed again, that I would happily die beneath this thin cotton sheet, sweating out my guilt and insecurity, listening to the tourists and birds chirp and squawk and sing.

I thought this could all change when I realized in a fever and lethargy flash of insight that I was in the possession of a 1964 Emerson television and that this could be the answer to all my problems. I suppose this was one of those moments alcoholics would call a moment of clarity, or rather a scintillating moment of unclarity. Call it intuition, a wild hunch, strange prophecy, whatever you like, but at some time in my convalescence I convinced myself that I could turn my television into a translation machine that could be programmed, with my help, to do the work of Fischer's book. This moment of catharsis was like I had been walking in front of a black backdrop, a nebulous void, then suddenly I found myself in front of red, red, red—an electricity passed through me. Had I stuck my finger in an electric socket? I didn't remember doing this, but no matter, the running of the voltage was omni-present. The television wasn't even my possession; it belonged to the house, but this slight matter of ownership did not give me pause—I am a translator, for goodness sake! The thing that did give me pause was my mechanical tinkering abilities. I was a snuffling imbecile when it came to electronic circuitry, but I vowed to not let a little lack of experience and proclivity, and fear slow me down. No, I dove right in and ripped off the back of the television; it came off surprisingly easy like a hard-boiled egg peeled at just the right spot. The wire switching, soldering, reconnection, hexing and voodoo work was another thing entirely. This was less like baking and more an intuitive act of electricianship. I mentioned this to Beatrice when the yellow phone jangled and it was her. She said electricity isn't something you want to approximate. I said, you may be right, but translation sure is—in fact, it's all just a little approximation and guessing and soldering game. Why not insert a little electricity into the already tenuous equation? I forget what she said in response, because I had important work to do and no time to waste.

Is this thing even on? I checked the connection, but the 1964 Emerson remained dark. At one time, it had at least fuzzed static, but now it stayed blank.

The television flickered softly. It was simply sleeping and it was my task to wake it up so it could assist me. I possessed the unexplainable hypothesis that the device would only work in the few moments before dawn, an electrical rooster of sorts, and thus I had been waking up before dawn for the past week in hopes of finding the device alive and humming with colors, scrolling words across its screen in a flicker of broadcast brilliance, leaving me to only quickly copy the sentences before they ran off the screen and back into the ether. But this was never the case, only ever a cruel static. The deadline was fast approaching; Alex would soon call for the first installment of *Hubbard's Return* and I had practically nothing for him. His s(e)izable advance was paying for my life on the island and in return I was staring at a 1964 Emerson television in hopes that it would produce my elusive translation, leaving me only to transcribe its fluency. Lunacy, undoubtedly, and I knew it, yet I believed in ghosts, Coleridge's opium induced vision that spawned "Kubla Khan" and even, in theory, Yeat's automatic writing experiments, especially if any of these yielded results.

And so I stared at the television. If the task of the

translator is to produce an echo of the original, I hoped to see the echo manifest on the screen in front of me, perhaps even to also hear the text, its inner cadences and rhythms. That would be good. I waited, patiently, but ultimately what I thought I desired never appeared. It was something else that arose.

It didn't work. Not at all. Not like I thought. I stared at the static. What time was it? 1:30 am? 4 am? I didn't know, somewhere near there. Had I eaten anything? Couldn't remember. Was I hungry? Should I eat? Probably, but I didn't feel like it. Some yogurt probably would've been good for my digestion, but sounded so goddamn boring. I wanted a blue cheese burger with oven fries or nothing. So I got nothing. I could feel large chunks of time slip behind my slow eyelids. Floating, floating. Flicker. Nothing. Then, the dim beginnings of a voice.

Fischer gave me precise but complicated directions to his house in that voice of his, the crazily assured voice of his book. I followed the directions without question; instead of getting on a train to Cardiff as I had first supposed, I got on another headed to Lance. Lost somewhere, I called him again to ask for help. He was overcome with laughter, saying, "Now you're really fucked, Roberto. You're lost." No matter, I said, I'll turn around and go home. He responded, "But you're never going to be able to go home, Roberto. Never." He had no idea where I was or how I could find my way back in order to keep my appointment with him. His voice reverberated in my ear long after I slammed down the earpiece to the payphone. I had been carrying a tan suitcase whose clasps had broken years ago in a dispute over a line from Chateaubriand, but I still hauled it with me on all my appointments because its compartments so well accommodated my books. I checked the suitcase in a locker at the train station, and since I had hours before a return train, I set out to walk around the small country town. The cobblestones gave way to redemptive alleys, light posts and large windows sadly open to the street. In one of these windows, I noticed it had become dark, streetlights in constellations. In another, I saw a bookshelf lit softly with track lighting. The spines were dark, titles and authors ghosted, and as I stared at the books, faces flashed before my eyes at vertiginous speeds, the faces I most admired, those I loved, imitated, envied and immolated in my mind's eye, the faces I protected, those I impaled, the faces I hardened myself against and those I sought in vain. And suddenly in the aftermath I remembered my suitcase back in the train station, and knew I had to return for it before my own face disappeared.

"Things are always on the move, simultaneously," Fischer whispers me, and I can hear the subtle wigglings of his tongue, so that any attempt to pinpoint the original is futile, shifting sand across the shadow country, the beach near Sagaponack where Fischer and I walk with his golden retriever, the beach grass and dunes, the tennis ball he pitches beyond sight, only to have it returned to him moments later, wet and excited and ready to go out again. Tall and craggy, Fischer speaks of the book we will work on together. "There's hardly a sentence in the whole damn thing that doesn't change, alter its meaning in some way since the last time I read it, let alone since I wrote it so many years ago."

Fischer tells me to steal, lie and cheat, whatever I think necessary. That's the only way to do it. What do you mean? I ask him– what are you saying? Steal it. Make it your own. I don't give a damn.

I sit down at my desk, the place where I'd been unable to complete anything, and without looking at the original, I begin to work, words flowing from my pen, Fischer's book scrolling out in front of me, gaining momentum, its own timbre, its own creases. The sentences are so beautiful. I've never seen ones like them before in my life. I don't even know from whom or from where they're coming.

A Response to These Disappearances

At a thankful height, we began to emerge. We'd been quiet half an hour through the woods. The horse's hooves sucked no sound on the brown soft track under the pines. But now, the land thinned and stretched before us. It must have taken some daring so many years ago by Father to put the wooden house where it was, tucked below and so obviously subservient to the mighty pasture land that stretched out and up before us in its long patches of craggy stone mended together by strips of green.

The wagon slowed. I looked up to where sky settled upon rock.

History presented herself to me as she always had, but this time I was ready for her. The dead could take a final form, but the living remain unformed, like myself, still in the making and susceptible, if we aren't careful, to shaping at the rough hands of the dead.

Up on the hill, descending, the single and intense image of Father, staff in hand. They called him The Shepherd of the Sorrento Plain. I heard his voice in time: "That's where we've lacked sense; our Bibles have taught us that what sheep need is a shepherd."

That very well may be, and I was never one to contradict Father, but suddenly I saw that a region of what I had thought gray stones was slowly moving as if the sun was making my eyesight unsteady. The wolves had arrived, a sea of fur and teeth and slink. I knew they'd never come closer.

Father, despite all his contradictions, had always stood clear. But Mother was a mystery. What drew her on? The main problem of history is how to approach a person of great importance who, having departed us too soon, left no telling. It expands. She expanded people into forms who could outlive her, expanded herself into the sleek creatures now bending my eyes. All ghosts are gray.

There was a kind of fold, she'd called it, up there in a sheltered spot high into the pasture land, and she'd slept up there in a shed she built herself for lambing time when the poor foolish creatures hurt themselves. That was what I wanted to see. It was still there, a little older and sagging, like all of us, but remained sturdy. I sat in it and thought about my parents, their bulk and mist, what they left to me, what I'd given them. There is no such thing as an equal exchange. I let the wolves surround me. I could smell them. They were all that was left, the wolves and the mind.

At last we were in the high wagon again. The old white horse had rested and soon we began to climb the long hill toward the hooded ridge. I held his hand. The road was new to me, as roads always are, going back.

FALL OF AN USHER

I'd never before been hired to be an usher, but when I received an offer from the vague Craigslist ad I'd replied to, I decided to go for it. What did I have to lose? I sure needed the money, and a drive north to Deer Isle seemed like a perfect way to spend a weekend in fall.

I'd sincerely thought the advertisement a scam when I first noticed it. Without any pictures or otherwise identifying logos or markers or even a name, the ad simply read: "Ushers needed for weekend wedding on Deer Isle. Will compensate fairly + gas + food. Responsible young men only." My roommate thought it was a thinly veiled sex ad. Others must've felt the way my roommate did, because I don't think the post's author received many replies. Someone returned my query within the hour, saying that I was hired, sending me an address to which I was to report on Friday night where my duties as usher would begin during the rehearsal dinner. The email included a cell phone number, but no name.

Before I left to drive north that Friday afternoon, my roommate said to me, "Don't you think there's a chance you're walking into a trap by some perverted homesteader Maine coon cats who are planning to use you for your body and then bury you in a silver box?" She raised her eyebrow like she'd just posed a rhetorical question meant to be philosophically debated. I didn't respond, instead pouring myself coffee into my travel mug. "I'm just worried about you, Kyle," she said. "That's sweet," I said, twisting the mug cap tight, "but I meet all the job criteria: young (youngish—check); responsible (enough); male (yep); and the underlying requirement, desperate (checkeroo)."

~

Like a fool, I punched my destination on Deer Isle into my cigarette-lighter plug-in GPS device and commenced brooding and driving, both mindless activities that felt more like the actions of an autopilot, interrupted periodically by a computerized womanly voice saying, "turn left in a quarter mile...turn around, if you can...turn around...turn around..." By the time I realized the GPS had been driving me in useless loops all over Blue Hill and Brooklin because, despite its disarmingly confident tone, it was completely befuddled, I had absolutely no earthly idea where I was or where I wanted to go. I had been so far down the thought hole of self-pity that I'd neglected to pay even the slightest attention to where I'd been driving. I yanked the GPS out of the dash and hurled it into the backseat, vowing to myself that I would never again use that stupid shitbox, though of course I could no longer count the amount of times I'd made the same vow, only to soon relapse into techno-addiction. I pulled off onto the gravelly shoulder of some pine-treed, unnamed blank road, put my hazards on, noticed that it was quickly getting dark, and dove into the back seat in search of the Gazetteer my father had given me three years ago upon my move south to the city. "You'll need this," he said, "I guarantee. Don't lose it!" Sadly, as I rummaged and continued to rummage, I realized I'd defied his advice and had indeed lost the atlas.

I experienced the brutally quick sensation of my world closing in on me, and the feeling of expansion I'd felt upon departure had been thrown too into the black hole of my backseat, along with the incompetent GPS and the ghost Gazetteer.

"Where the holy hell are you?" The voice in my head could've been that of the digitized travel diva, or it could've been my father's, as he indeed would've reveled in my stupidity, but in fact, the voice was mine.

Then, in a flash of gratitude, I remembered the cell phone number buried at the bottom of my employer's email. I tried to pull it up on my phone, but of course I couldn't get any service up here in God-Knows-Where Isle. This was the point I began to cry. I don't really know why. I was fine, had plenty of gas, and probably had a half-stale bag of chips in the backseat that would sustain me if necessary. However crying felt like the thing to do, and so I did it with abandon, big wholesale sobs, head down on the steering wheel. It felt good.

At some point—it could've been five minutes or two hours—I realized it was now completely dark and I was due at the rehearsal dinner in about a half hour. I decided to simply drive forward, drive on, and trust that something good would happen. This is basically how I lived my life at this time, and it had worked well enough up until then. Actually, who am I kidding? That philosophy worked horribly. I was miserable and desperately trying to escape the pain of my life, desperately trying to avoid dealing with the string of hurt I'd been wracking up. So, no, that philosophy hadn't actually been working, but unfortunately, at this point, I didn't see my other options. I drove.

I hadn't been driving for more than two minutes before I heard my phone beep. Somehow, I'd miraculously driven into service range, and when I looked at my phone, it was a text from my roommate: "Where r u?" I pulled over, texted back "Bumblefuck, ME", found my employer's phone number, called it, and discovered I was about ten minutes away from the rehearsal dinner. Who needs a Gazetteer, I rebutted my father's voice, when you have dumb luck?

~

It was completely dark when I arrived at the house where the rehearsal dinner was taking place. I couldn't see enough to even know where to park. My employer said it would be obvious. It wasn't. It felt like I was taking a left turn from the road into either a pond or a field. Luckily it was a field. I crunched gravel up a slight incline, rounded a slight bend and the house was above me. However, "house" isn't the right term, more like mansion or estate or palace. The huge stone façade was ground lit so that from my inclined approach, it seemed to lean over me like a Duke's funhouse. I knocked with the large brass knocker and the thick walnut door swung open. Someone handed me a tray and a bow tie, and I was off, walking and working, attuned to the immediate hum of the dinner, the murmuring of the guests, more of a dull roar, though in retrospect, when I lay in my bed later that night, I couldn't remember a single face of any guest. They all blurred into suited shoulders, exposed necklines, a glimmering necklace all without a face. Or rather, the faces were a river of fine features flowing quickly downstream and my memory unable to alight on any single one.

At the end of the night, when all tables had been folded up and all stray glasses collected in the kitchen, I stood in the back lawn, gazing out at what I'd been told was a stunning view of the ocean, but I couldn't see anything. Clouds completely hid the stars so that I could only assume that somewhere in my field of vision there was a patch of sky and a patch of ocean, but where that dividing line scratched itself out horizontal I had no idea. I'd snuck enough sips of wine over the course of the night to be more than a little tipsy, so that gazing out into this unsteady night only served to disorient me, and as my head swam, I had the sudden urge to vomit.

I felt a tap, tap, tapping on my shoulder by someone's insistent finger. I spun around a little too quickly and my head wasn't able to catch up. I almost fell over when I looked back toward the house still ablaze with lights. Silhouetted against the house I saw a figure, most likely a woman with a high-collared coat. Thank you for your services tonight, young man, she said in some indistinct but refined accent. We'll expect you at the chapel by noon tomorrow; you'll have quite a few duties to perform, but we'll make it worth your while.

She left, and left me with a distinct feeling of dread. I couldn't articulate what felt wrong, but something did. The woman reminded me of a Cruella DeVille type and I felt like I would get what I deserved for selling myself to such people, but did that thought stop me? Of course not.

My room in the hostel was more of a portioned-off area in a field. So many night noises that threatened my sleep. Before I finally dropped off, I saw a text from my roommate. "How was the dinner?" In a moment of sleep-addled honesty, I replied, "Fine. Lil' drunk. Have bad feeling, but probably just nerves." I didn't hear back from my roommate that night. I slept fitfully, plagued by terrible nightmares of the ground opening up in the middle of the night that was so dark I couldn't do anything other than fall forward into the chasm whose bottom I never encountered.

The morning curled itself around me, a chilly fog, and the coffee tasted unbelievably good, so dark and delightfully bitter that I was surprised that any public house would dare make coffee so bold. But indeed, as had been a theme of this journey, no one else seemed to be staying at the hostel. I didn't even see an innkeeper or a grounds person, but someone had put out the homemade danishes that accompanied the coffee, of which I partook more than I probably should've, but they practically melted in my mouth with a buttery give away. Before I knew it, the fog burned off and it was already almost eleven o'clock. I needed to get into my tuxedo and make my way to the Wintercrest Chapel.

People milled about outside of the chapel. They looked normal to me and I felt a wave of relief pass over, for I still entertained the unconscious possibility that the people who'd attend this wedding weren't people at all, and instead were zombies or some soulless variety of marauders. But no, they were real people somberly but festively dressed. A woman called to me and I recognized her as the woman from the rehearsal dinner last night, but she lacked the Cruella DeVille high cape, instead looking completely normal and in fact, she reminded me a little of my grandmother crossed with Barbara Streisand. She directed me to my place at the entrance to the tiny chapel, showed me the basket of programs I was to hand out and finally showed me the bucket of white rice I was to offer handfuls to guests as they left the chapel. As I ran my hand through the rice, letting it grain cascade through my fingers, I noticed a very large worm wriggling through the basket, trying to burrow its way deeper to the bottom. I dug out the worm and flicked it into the grass outside the chapel, relieved that my keen observation had saved the wedding from the potentially embarrassing act of throwing a large worm on the bride's perfect dress. Little did I know that I'd never have the opportunity to offer this rice to the wedding guests.

The interior of the Wintercrest Chapel remained as it probably existed at the turn of the 19th Century. Punched tin ceiling and wainscoting, high back wooden pews, long thin stained glass windows, wide pine floorboards. The entire chapel had been tastefully and sparsely filled with pine boughs. It was, quite simply, one of the most aesthetically pleasing, beautiful interiors I could call to mind.

I assumed my position at the door and people filed in. I handed out the programs, glancing at one in the interim between guests. I thought I must've been mistaken, but in that brief glimpse, I thought I saw printed: "We celebrate the Union of Day & Night," which seemed very odd to me. Maybe it was some kind of joke, maybe nicknames, or hypocorisms, "ol' Bill, we call him Mr. Night." Or something like that. Or maybe it was the couples' last names: Mr. Night and Ms. Day would soon become, what, Mr. and Mrs. Night, Mr. and Mrs. Day, Day-Night? I continued passing out programs because it was my job and I felt I had to do it.

Then the chapel was full of people and I was given the signal to sit down. I found a place in one of the back pews. I took my phone out of my pocket, silenced it and placed it on the pew beside me. A tall man, obviously the Preacher, motioned to everyone in welcome and began to speak. As he did so, from the left side of the chapel, a man dressed in a completely black tuxedo took his place on the small stage. A few moments later, from the right side of the stage, a woman in a long flowing white dress appeared.

The Preacher said, "Are there any among you who find objection in the marriage today of Day to Night, the holy union of Light and Dark?"

Into the silence preceding this question, I burst out laughing, an unqualified, unpardonable guffawing screech like someone had slipped a bucketful of squirming worms down my pants. Every head in the chapel turned to look at me. I felt mortified, but couldn't help myself. "You, sir, in the back," the Preacher said, "do you have an objection? It is now your time to step forward."

I found myself rising to my feet and walking to the front of the chapel to stand next to the Preacher. All eyes must've been boring holes into me, but I failed to notice. "I have an objection," I heard myself say, but even now after all that's happened, I don't know why I did this. "The Day should be forbidden from wedding the Night. It is unconscionable, it is an act of incest, an unholy union of Brother and Sister."

That is the last thing I remember.

I awoke in a hospital bed. My roommate sat in a

chair beside my bed. When she saw I was awake, she said, "Good afternoon, sunshine. There you are. I didn't know if you were going to make it for a while."

I looked down the length of my body to find it swathed in white bandages.

"Where did you meet those people, Kyle?"

"Craigslist."

"Well, there you go. Do you even know what just happened to you?"

My face felt like what I imagined a face would feel like immediately following delux botox. When my expression remained expressionless, my roommate said, "Let me tell you what just happened to you."

You utter your objections to the wedding like a fool, not knowing what you do. The Preacher, who is not a preacher, throws a burlap sack over your head. The groom, who is not a groom, pushes you to the floor. The bride, who is not a bride, kicks you in the head—you can feel the bump now—and almost knocks you out. The Preacher pulls a box of matches from somewhere within his robes, douses your burlaped form with gasoline, lights a match and drops it on you. Your body, even though you're almost unconscious, reacts against the terror and you throw your body around the stage, bucking and fighting against the flames. This must've been amazingly vigorous because somehow you thrash your way over to a bucket for an especially large bouquet of pine boughs, knocking it over and into a fire extinguisher that somehow—don't ask me how—goes off and foams out your fire.

I blink at my roommate. She must've registered my disbelief.

"Yes, this all really happened. The smoke sets off the fire alarms, which causes everybody in the 'wedding' party to flee, leaving your smoldering body for the fire department to find. The police are looking for the wedding people, but they doubt they'll find them. I'd left Portland that morning and I was almost here when I got a call from the police because I was the last number in your phone. They told me to come directly to the hospital."

She looked at me haltingly. "I want to hold your hand, touch you somewhere, but there isn't any place that's not burned."

I held her with my eyes. She started to cry.

"I'll take care of you, you know. I will. You know that, don't you?"

I wanted to say yes, but I couldn't. I tried to shift my weight in her direction, but the pain was incredible, more pain than I ever thought possible. I registered the fabric rustle of the stiff hospital sheets before I blacked out.

When I woke up, she was still there.

Perhaps the Sea

Only the steady creaking of a flight of swans
disturbed the silence, labouring low over head
with outstretched necks towards the sea.
— *The Fox in the Attic*, Richard Hughes

A mbrose was absolutely alone with it in his grandfather's huge, empty house. He dumped it on the big dust-sheeted living room sofa, left it there, and hurried across the silent hall to wash his shifting hands. As he walked his property he'd recently inherited from his grandfather, he'd found it in the north pasture among the brambles beyond a copse of hemlock about a hundred yards from the Contoocook. He didn't even know what it was, but he knew he felt an obligation to bring it back with him to Fuller Road slung like a slipping yoke across his shoulders. Ambrose had never seen anything like it in his entire life. Its clouded outer covering reminded him of a sea, but how he knew this he could not say. The object caused him to age as if he'd been carrying it from the quiet north pasture for his thirty years and in the meantime he'd found himself passed from a boy attending the Meeting School to a middle-aged man who found himself alone in this farmhouse, benefactor to the decrepit but stately air.

He called for the examiner, as someone would have to come examine his discovery, but the regular examiner had suffered a fall from a horse and would be laid up for at least a week. The Central Agency said they would send another lady from Exeter as soon as they could, but it might be later in the week.

Ambrose put on a kettle. Today was only Monday. He warmed himself in front of the fire. The thing still lay stretched across the sofa beside him. From the armchair, he watched how the fire's reflection danced and shimmered across its folded form. Again, for the hundredth time that day, he wondered what it was and why it was that he felt so affected. The water was boiling and he rose to the kettle.

A gift, that's how Ambrose thought of it, something he'd not even known was coming to him, but a change now seemed to have seeped into him, for he found he doubted his desire for this gift. It felt like too much for Ambrose to hold, too much expanse like the panic some feel when viewing a great desert.

The night was now well along and he went out walking in it.

This particular night, like one he might find stranded and abandoned at the height of day, felt melancholic as if it had incurred a wound of unknown origin and no matter what manner of healing Ambrose envisioned, no matter what path or stitch he traced, the wound would never heal, and in fact such a wound was never meant to heal. Rather, for one out walking in such a night, it nicked tiny corresponding wounds in a body that resembled silver tears. And so Ambrose was struck. Sleep overcame him somewhere in the north pasture not far from where he'd found it. Under the log he usually lay beneath, he curled his body.

When the sun lit him, Ambrose awoke covered in a light dew. A slight chill lay on the top level of his body and to dispel this he rose and began to walk. He had a sudden premonition that the examiner would arrive that morning and he must immediately return home.

The examiner arrived as Ambrose had just turned onto Fuller Road. He rode with her in her small car from the start of the road the nearly quarter of a mile to the farmhouse.

The car pulled up in front of the garage, coming to rest on the blanket of pine needles that covered almost all of the ground around the garage. They sat in the car beneath the basketball hoop mounted at a sag above the garage doors. Ambrose could count on one hand the times he'd shot baskets here.

Ambrose hung the examiner's coat and cap in the front closet. He knew she wouldn't expect much from him in the way of hospitality, but he desired to make an effort.

No need bothering with the kettle, Mr. Fuller. I'll get working straight away. Where is it?

Ambrose turned on the light that lead to the living room.

Now if you'd give me some time alone, the examiner requested with a quiet smile.

Ambrose retired to the kitchen. What seemed like

hours passed, but could've only been a few minutes. The afternoon was still, but approached evening.

When the examiner emerged, she found Ambrose still in the kitchen. Perhaps now would be a time for a nice cup of tea, she said. As the water's temperature rose, they sat in silence. He poured the water from the kettle. She sipped gingerly for a moment before speaking.

From what I can tell, it seems to be a swan of some kind, though one I've never seen before, an ancient one or perhaps a lost breed. It also seems to have been damaged by foxes, I would imagine, for he has wounds all over his white, but at the moment, he is alive. And in fact, as evidenced from the slight flutter of his forehead, I'd say he's dreaming, a rare thing for a creature so damaged. It is my best opinion as an examiner that he is dreaming of the sea, although I cannot logically say why I feel confident of this. Perhaps the sea is a return to something, a place or a time long past. I don't completely know, but he may yet heal from this. My advice is to continue to let him sleep, and when he wakes, if he awakes, do your best to see him to the skies.

Now, if you don't mind, Mr. Fuller, I'd like my coat, please. It's getting late in the day and soon all the whiteness will be gone.

Ambrose Fuller had not been to the sea in some months, not since his grandfather had died. In his professional career, his grandfather Bruce was a land surveyor for the state of New Hampshire, and over the course of his eighty-nine years, he patiently acquired the neighboring land around his modest farmhouse along the Contoocook, enough land that as a little boy Ambrose had nightmares of losing himself within his grandfather's tracts of land. Ambrose, in his teenage years, came to know this land through walking it with Bruce in order to check the fox box-traps that dotted the land. To say that his grandfather had been obsessed with foxes would have been an understatement. "A fox is a wolf who sends flowers," Bruce used to tell Ambrose and there were not words to describe the effect finding a fox had on Bruce. The only way Ambrose could describe this was that finding a fox was like Bruce somehow returned home. Bruce never did anything other than commune with the foxes for a few moments before freeing them. He whispered to them through the cage. To calm them, he told Ambrose, to listen to their hearts. I give them a mantra. Bruce never told Ambrose the mantra, but was it Ambrose's imagination that the foxes seemed calmer the moment Bruce spoke to them?

Now that land belonged to Ambrose. There were others in his family who wanted things, as always, but the land was his. However what he would do with it was unknown.

Ambrose made his way to the sea. The swan, who had slowly but miraculously healed itself, was sleeping in a cage in the back of Ambrose's truck. He drove to the nearest coastal city. It was an overcast day with the clouds hanging low to the horizon like a quilted ceiling. There were moments, as he wheeled his truck through the streets of the small city, that he caught a glimpse of the sea, just a shimmering glint of light off water, far off at first, but yet the undulating texture unmistakable. And there were signs for it, directing Ambrose with arrows and place names. He followed the signs and could feel himself descending in altitude, subtly drawing closer to the zero point. He hummed a quiet song to himself, a graceful melody of fire and loss. He tapped his thumbs on the steering wheel, then leaned to one side as his arms turned the wheel, his foot working the brake, his breath steady and deep, his eyes scanning the wharves beyond the windshield. Rolling down the window, he could smell the salt.

MIDNIGHT

My grandfather, James Patrick O'Donehue, was called Midnight by everyone from his fellow longshoremen to his daughters to Father Brown. He'd joined the Portland Longshoremen in 1889, nine years after its inception. He worked at the Grand Trunk Depot, loading and unloading Canadian grain onto the beltway that connected all the wharves. By the time I interviewed Pupup for the book a history professor from St. Joe's was writing on the Irish longshoremen, he was eighty-seven, three more years to live. With his graveled voice from his wheelchair, he said, for this call me Midnight. He'd gotten the nickname because he always worked the late shifts, but had the energy of eight a.m. black coffee. I was spry, he said, and I could see the holes in his mouth.

Commercial Street. The Grand Trunk. Harbor Fish. Lehman's. His pleasure arose from the feeling that these places meant something to him that they no longer did to most people, as if the names were old friends with whom he had experienced much; he smiled as his lips shaped the sounds and found memories of himself in their pronunciation.

They all knew ol' Midnight was a hellraiser, handsprings and upper cuts. Skull dragging what felt like a half ton of grain. But never stopped. No weather, nor heartache. Always to work.

Midnight coughed phlegm and blood into a paper cup he always kept with him. At least you felt alive then without all these hours around you. It's so quiet here—he points to his skull—you can hear the birds flying. Sound like ghosts. My memory flying away on wings. I go to bed so early now. Nowhere near Midnight.

What about when you joined into The International Longshoremen's Association? Yeah, there was that. And he talks for a few moments. Pauses. Spits. Asks me for a glass of water. Would rather have whiskey. Winks. What were we talking about, my boy, nice you want to know about these things. Most people don't care. Memories stay up here until they fly away. Like birds you know.

Why were you called 'longshoremen'? Midnight resumes as one takes up a refrain for a song. Because we worked along the shore, boy, along the shore.

An Absence in the Mouth

The baby was a normal baby, except he was born with teeth. His parents split up soon after he was born.

Teeth are unjust things. They rattle and crow inside us. The boy grew. His teeth did not seem unusual in any way other than they were simply there. His mother often ran her fingers over the ends of her baby's teeth. They were so sharp, weren't they so sharp? Luckily it seemed that though her son indeed possessed authentic teeth in his small mouth, he did not know yet how to use them. Nursing felt like wading thigh deep into a lake for a few minutes as tiny fish nipped ungently at her.

One never knows what sort of child one will receive. The boy took to biting at an early age, and bit other children with such savagery that he attracted the attention of the priest in the parish where his mother was a lax parishioner and where the boy attended preschool. The priest kindly pulled aside the boy's mother, who was mortified and had always feared, with the boy's past, that something like this would happen.

However, rather than the rebuke the mother expected, the priest mentioned an admiration for the boy's intensity, certainly a quality the boy had in abundance. Your son, the priest said in a hushed tone, is — he murmured something in Latin that she couldn't understand—then he walked away as if entranced.

The boy, as most boys do, grew out of the biting, and then he embarked upon a relatively normal childhood. However, when he began to lose his baby teeth, which of course had been with him since the moment of his birth, the boy grew notably withdrawn. At some point, his mother noticed with alarm that he hadn't eaten in she didn't know how long. When she confronted him, he declared that he could no longer do it. He could no longer eat. His mother did not know what to do, and it was not her imagination that the boy began to lose weight, his cheekbones shining through his face like ping pong balls in poor light.

The mother, after a prolonged period of willful forgetting, remembered what the priest had said on the playground that day many years ago, and though she did not understand it, she'd never forgotten his words. She visited the church in an attempt to find the priest, though she hadn't attended the church since that interaction on the playground years ago. Father D'Avalo was dead, an elderly lady told the mother. He'd died one year ago this spring. How did he die, the mother asked, afraid. He died of an infection. A rare one. A sudden one. From a nasty dog bite. How strange you should ask now. There is going to be a remembrance this week in the cathedral on State Street.

The mother decided to attend the remembrance, and to try to bring along her son, who these days did nothing but lie around the house staring blankly at his toys. With a little cajoling, he surprisingly agreed to accompany his mother to the service. On the drive there, the mother, as she often did, asked her son if he was hungry. "Starving" was the word he tried to say. By now he'd lost all his baby teeth and his mouth was a pink gum cave. Everything folded in on itself. Can you try a grape? His mother had brought them along. He shook his head. How about a smoothie? She could tell he wanted to, but he simply couldn't.

The remembrance was in the afternoon in the central nave of the large cathedral that nobody ever went to anymore. There was a smattering of gray heads in the first few pews. A woman approached the altar, stood on the short stage, and turned to face the audience.

We all miss the father, the woman said, without introducing herself. We are lost without him. He left us too early. But we all remember him.

The mother turned to sneak a glimpse of her son. He was weeping.

But we must continue without him, the woman said. We must live on in his name. Make his hunger our hunger, make his heart our heart. At that moment, a sense of pure relief spread over the mother because she'd saved her son's baby teeth, though her first instinct had been to get rid of the white knives. Why did she feel this? She knew in that moment her son would never again possess teeth.

The son lived another eleven years. Not a long life by any means, but long enough. He had dreams. Some of them came true, but like all of us, many did not. But the boy never ate another bit or drop or spoonful of food in his life. I just can't, he'd mouth. Doctors gave him three months to live, then six, then, surely, one year; the point of his body's expiration, like a universe, kept expanding. The boy, now a young man, lived to disprove, an exception. Some thought him a hero. None of it mattered to the boy born with teeth. None of it.

His mother had the misfortune of outliving her son. No one should have to do that, but after a while, it wasn't going to be a surprise. She'd been watching it come closer and closer since the day the boy was born. When he died, his mother had him cremated and she put his ashes in an antique silver fruit bowl with a lid. To his ashes, she added what she'd always saved: his teeth. She sprinkled them into the bowl. They plopped with a dry poof, then she mixed them in with a wooden spoon. There he was, all of him, her hungry, hungry boy.

The True Outskirts of Home

The darkness deepened more desolate for the dull bright glow of the kitchen candles.

Burning down now. Almost gone.

The noises in the night were like the chirps and squawks of birds I'd seen some long time ago in one of Altman's drawings.

A woman sat across from me. We'd met that afternoon. She knew an old friend.

"Forgive me," Pat said, "I didn't mean offense."

We were quiet. She sipped her decaf as if she were one of the aforementioned birds of night, sipping the blackness. I held my cup of chamomile with both hands and sat back against the chair with my legs beneath me. Pat looked up to the wall above my head. "Bluebird," she said, "who painted that snowscape?"

I turned my head to be able to see the painting as if I didn't know its every texture and tone.

My face, the face I have in extremity.

That was all there was. That was the evocation: a small spasm of memory that could never fully elucidate itself, a woman who stared too long at a distant shape and could not be sure if it moved or lay still.

Pat, who will now disappear from the story, continued to sip and each time she lowered her cup, the cat peered into it.

I decided I wanted to tell the story. Yes, I wanted to, for no other reason than to hear it told, hear myself tell it. I knew that someday in the not too distant future the story would be forgotten. Altman and I, we left no remnants of our love, we chose it like that, and we knew, if only unconsciously, what would happen because of this choice. We put our story in the hands of a listener; in this case it was Pat, a woman who I was not interested in beyond her ability to become a vessel.

"We were a house of women," I began.

But that is not the way it will now appear.

VI. Winter 1985

I never took Altman to have Madam Shirley read our palms, probably because I was afraid, because I knew that Madam Shirley would read some truth about me, about us, in Altman's hand. Altman was always a frightful mirror, and what we called love was perhaps nothing more than my standing in front of her holding a blue flower while she held two small candles in a gust of terrible winter that burst from beneath the crack of the cabin door. So I never took Altman to Madam Shirley's. Also because I knew she'd hate it. I hate that shit, she'd say and pretend to gag herself with her index finger. Then she'd go back outside to her studio.

Before Altman, I was a social person, or at least I had

the potential to be. But after we'd been living together in the cabin for a few months, I never saw anybody else besides Altman, never felt like it. Maybe a few people when in town for groceries. But even then people'd look at me askance like I was feral. Or a fool. Like I had 'forbidden' tattooed across my forehead.

My father never visited. It would've all eventually reconciled itself. He would've gotten over it and come out. It couldn't have been any other way. But then the accident like bloodstains inexpertly removed.

Altman could physically do anything she wanted. Chopped wood for hours. Taught me how. Repaired anything. Carried the heaviest. Our divisions simply fell like that. No other way it could've been. No other way to want it. I loved the ancient gas stove. It was like the stove wove a magic tapestry of flavor and love around anything I cooked in or on it.

Altman and the snowmobile. It gave her a thrill to speed and bounce over pocked snow, grooves flashing gray, bruised light of winter towards town. We had to have a snowmobile. No other way to get to the cabin once snow. We kept Altman's truck down a mile in Rawn's barn. He never charged us nothing.

My washing. I remembered it. And a sudden strip of crushed light split earth from sky. That's how I knew. It went straight into my brain like a shunt.

This cabin I am living in now resembles that former one in every way: the slant of its one room, the smell of interior wood, a good bit of stale sweat, the exact same furniture, the morning light that bends and becomes attenuated at noon time, overlaps the afternoon. Everything is the same, even the path to the door, whatever the season, the surrounding trees like friends and those few stones that make up the path that Altman built.

These hours and minutes of time also resemble the hours and minutes of my own life. I talk. To people. In the moment in which they spin around me, I tell myself: "They seem real. How much they seem like real people!"

My face, sometimes reflected in an inevitable window, returns a version of me. With insistence. I see someone who looks like me. Yes very much. I recognize her.

But after all, no one must think it actually is me.

Altman had gone for wood. She'd taken the snowmobile. Cold. We didn't want to run out. She hadn't been gone long, but I knew. My washing. I put on my boots and went out.

I found her in the snow. She'd fallen off the snowmobile. Altman's hands still clenched to her heart. She'd told me about her heart, but the way she worked, I never would've thought…I pulled her back to the cabin.

On the way back, her weight. Crows, a murder of them all gathered on a bare tree. Calling to me, look there, a poem by Maria Sabina transformed into crows. And there, two lines from Octavio Paz, thighs of the sun, corners of a forgotten summer.

The same body belongs to me. I use these same eyes that cloud over or squint shut to see a bright sunset.

I took her home. That was what I did.

V. Spring 1983

I watched Altman in the rain. The backside of the studio had blown off during the previous night, and she was determined to fix it, no matter the weather. Or at least shore up the damage. She trembled in her raincoat, straining to lift a mass of fallen branches and I imagined she felt the separate stuff of her clothes hung heavy with water.

As she worked to rectify, a soup sat to simmer on the stove.

We'd been living happy for a while.

In these woods, it felt like the Paris I'd never seen but always wanted to. Altman, of course, would never stoop to the urban, let alone Europe. She'd go crazy and I knew it. It was uncomplicated in that way. I allowed it to be so. In the quickest moments of love, when Altman's belly arced above me, I would suffer loss, and relish it. It was a comfortable sacrifice that became easy as it grew beyond the frightful lucidity of the convalescent, or the smooth repetition of the perfectly stupid athlete.

"There isn't any time for the world to miss you, Bluebird," Altman said as she left for the morning with an axe in her hand. "Go to your Paris, wherever. I'm not keeping you.'

But we both knew I wouldn't go. I loved the talk of the foreign, but I would never invite it within me.

So we began to walk about in our own fabulous Paris, letting ourselves be guided by the nighttime signs, following routes born of deer and moose.

Our cabin lit up in the darkness of a night walk's end, and we stopped in confidential glens to kiss on fallen trees, hopscotch across a pine-padded floor, those childish rites of love and a hop on one leg Home.

Altman spoke of fish, leaf, cloud, image, unless she did not speak at all.

An image in a painting.

"The idiots always say we have to believe them," Altman said and then she blew smoke rings. The pinks and blues lay dormant in the earth, let alone the full prestige of green. But soon.

In the afternoons we used to go see the fish in Meyer's Pond in March the frog month, the crouching month. A warming sun on occasion took a little more bare earth each day. From the bench pondside, paying no attention to the flies, we would wait for the moment when we could see the fish bubbles. We went slow. All the bubbles out in the sun. The moment before they burst. Hung in the air, motionless birds in the round. An absurd joy would take us and we would sing, Altman dragging me across the grass to enter the world from below.

Air underneath the sun, spheres of water that mix with us. Pink and black birds dance softly, wings tickling our noses in a little chunk of air. Cold light birds. We would look at them, trying to bring our attention to the glass world, trying to touch it, annoying all the other animals. We understood less and less what a bird was. A fish. We proceeded along the path of not understanding, of ignorance, and getting closer to those creatures that did not seek to understand each other. We rolled among the bubbles and were close.

"Cold water kills them," I said. Altman nodded, bereft of words. "Cold water is a sad thing." And I remembered my father talking about a fern, "don't water it, put a plate of water under it, then when it wants to drink, it can, and when it doesn't want to, it doesn't..."

A single fish will get sad by itself.

The sky is a mirror.

The moments were delicious, delicate, her scent something like very thin chocolate and oranges. We were getting drunk on fruit and analogies. Our anuses. Always trying. And that perfect fish, do you remember? A fish the exact shade of a shadow of a violet piece of air.

We found out how life left off. Shapes without a third dimension disappeared when they faced me, left a motionless pink line. A flick of a fin and miraculous eyes. Her eyes. Whiskers. And a belly with a transparent ribbon coming out that did not come loose. No one could pluck or cut it. The perfection of pure imagery.

Excrement. We needed nothing more, which would only compromise us, to use one of those fine phrases we so liked to use in those days.

IV. SUMMER 1982

Father and I visited Altman at her cabin. Whatever his former anger, it had mollified enough so that he was concerned about her supplies for the upcoming winter in her single room cabin without electricity. My father wanted someone to help him with the hazard lantern and the cord of wood he was giving Altman, and even though I was a girl, I was his only option, as my brother Johnny had moved to Portland nine months ago to work retail. My father rolled his eyes when he said "retail" like he was infected.

Then, after a while, I started to come by myself.

At first I visited because I wanted Altman to bring me into her world, never consciously though, but bringing me in all the same because I was a person who wanted to escape the ordinary routine of Cars and History. And here, I thought, was someone who had.

During that initial visit with my father, I watched Altman and wondered what impulse worked on her. When I returned later, I began to know. In those quick moments, a vein of instinctive sanity opened and flowed: a warning that every desire must be redeemed in the end.

My father was off somewhere, maybe down by the truck. Altman stood with her hip against one of the front posts of the cabin. I held the hazard light clumsy in my hands. We looked at each other and I think it was then that she began to desire me. For me, it was earlier. She said something covered in misunderstandings that dissolved into a vague moment of silence until our hands began to talk, much later, sweet stroking hands while we rubbed each other with our eyes. We were in agreement. The world curled outside, still light late into evening. We were barely alive and nothing had a name or a history.

I watched her breath and her slight dream movements, skin so transparent that I imagined seeing through to her small, complex reproductive organs with their ability to change my world.

III. SPRING 1982

My father and Altman had an argument. I could tell by the way he stormed into the kitchen through the backdoor still holding the cans of white paint he'd intended to give Altman. He didn't mention anything to me about it. I was trying to read for class at the kitchen table while keeping an eye on a pot of rice. That night, after dinner, my father asked me to take the cans of paint out to Altman's studio in the hayloft of the barn at the edge of our property. I don't want to talk to her, maybe ever again, he said and went upstairs. I could tell he was upset because I heard the gentle whir of his electric razor, something he only did to soothe the rage. My father always had a very smooth face in anger. I was used to being a messenger between my father and Altman, very rarely the other way around. He often sent her supplies, plates of food, blankets. I avoided talking to Altman when I went out to the barn, which was easy, for Altman rarely spoke to me. Sometimes she grunted in thanks.

The hayloft received a startling amount of natural light during the day. By night, Altman rigged lights from beams. Books were piled around the room, stacked atop one another in places climbing to teetering heights. The books felt peripheral to the room, having nothing to do with Altman's center. In the incandescent light with the paint cans clutched in my hands like pullets and the antique densities of books behind her, Altman turned to look at me, twenty-two years old and floundering towards graduation. She said, there. Put them there. I did as I was told.

Then I waited. You can go now, Altman said and turned back to a canvas. She wore a thin white t-shirt, even though it almost felt cold enough for me to see my breath. I could see the outline of two wings protruding sharp from her back. She stood barefoot. Her feet were dirty. I paused for a moment longer, listening to my breath. And then I left.

II. Summer 1981

As one drives north toward Rockland, after finding Route 1 in Brunswick, one passes through, for less than half a mile, a gambit of pine trees that are so thick they appear to be netted together to form a seamless wall of boughs and needles.

The trees are so tall and dense that they look as if they have been cultivated for centuries. I have always watched for them. Driving north, they were the true outskirts of home. I never pointed them out to my father, never told him of their power for me. But when we drove through them, a few seconds, I prayed to them. This stretch of land was a time sanctuary for me and during its passing, I sometimes ran a list of my desires, my loves, my problems, and I prayed for their happy resolution. Other times during this gambit, I did nothing and instead allowed the pines to open me and extract what was most important to my soul, lift it into the light of prayer. In this way, space was acoustic, ringing out empty, shaping meaning, spreading silence out like a zeroed thing.

I never spoke during the pines and in fact sometimes, if I had been speaking, I would cease to speak, or cease to listen in order to more fully feel. No one knew this. Most of the time my silence was not imposed upon, but I remember one particular time it was.

I was driving with my father and we had been silent for a while when we entered the pines, then he spoke.

I've decided to invite Altman to live with us, he said, she can have the barn to work and sleep, we never use it. That was all he said. It was not a question for my approval, but rather a statement of the coming future. I didn't respond. We passed through the pines. Then I turned to him. Okay, I said, fine with me. There was nothing to object to. I thought I knew enough about Altman to know that she would pose no threat to me or my relationship with my father.

I. FALL 1980

My father was a high school English teacher for his entire life. My mother left us when I was three. I don't know where she went. Everything is about loss, but everyone knows that. My father wandered into a gallery on Main Street in Rockland one late morning. He saw a canvas scarred white with snow along one wall. His gaze rested, caught by its beauty. Who painted that, he asked. Roberta Altman.

The primary function of sight is to enslave human beings. Little holes break all over my vision. Widen and break. What do all the holes mean? All my attempts to reduce the number of holes feel so pitiful. Holes arrive and open continually. Arrive and open. What will it all look like later? Will I recognize any of it? What if I do not? It's difficult to say what the last thing was I saw. Truly saw.

THE VIBRATIONS OF HER LINES:
A SCENT MEMORY

Last year I was fortunate enough to spend some time in the coastal town of R. at the Captain Lindsay House, which stands a few hundred feet from the small and struggling waterfront. At one of the breakfasts, sitting next to a couple from the South on vacation to visit their daughter, I overheard that the Captain Lindsay House was for sale. The couple mentioned this fact briefly in passing, as if the uncertain fate of the Lindsay House reflected poorly on their judgment as discerning citizens of taste and class. Indeed, after that one morning at breakfast, I never saw the couple again.

The price was a million dollars, an amount whose rare and delectable scent I found impossible to analyze, for I rarely had more money than the sum total of rent, dinners at the tavern, a night or two away and a small cache for unforeseen but inevitable dental expenditures.

I went out walking and found myself not insignificantly depressed at the possibility that the great architectural heart of the Lindsay could be possessed by some frosted academy hell-bent on turning the waterfront into a campus (with authentic wharves + seagulls) for wealthy film students.

A salty blast swept through the broad waves of air, diluting without drowning my melancholy. The breakwater rose before me as a single expressive mass, a disembodied mouth, her teeth sunk into the sea and only her lips visible to the breaking waves.

Spray and the revelatory beauty of a single gull.

The supernatural violet of the sea rose as a pseudonym for an essence far too deep for me to discern.

Several days later, as I was nearing the end of my stay, I met a woman ascending the main staircase of the Lindsay, her face averted in a long, pink-black coat. Violet, as her name became, stayed in a lofty room above mine, and she smelled faintly of a delicious fragrance I was smelling for the first time, a blend of brackish reverence and floral perfume. Her scent closed the door on my up-until-then pervasive melancholy, a solemn and gentle closing. Vanishing into the vertical lines of her beauty felt like an ascendance into a unique school of air and dispossession.

One single time. A crack in tonality. Her vibrations disappearing into the adjoining room.

After she returned and lay beside me, Violet said, "I am in the process of buying the Captain Lindsay House." I could smell her.

I stood up and, reaching for the door handle, I realized the crush of her scent had made me mute. Love itself had abruptly arrived with its unexpected roses and jagged claws hooked into me. I stumbled out into the hallway.

"William! William!" Violet called after me. But it was too late. Love had blended itself with its immense breath and sculpting presence into everything around me. My melancholy, suddenly returned, was now infinite. What did I know about love? Did I know anything of its fragrance of sadness? No, not me. I did not know a thing.

And so I fled in search of a purer intensity, a kind of light work not possible there. And love, too, went away. But its weakened scent still hangs about the callow tips of my memory: a brackish wisp and the nostalgia of the body in high fever.

Rural Maine Crossroads, circa 1870

By the time Reverend Dinsmore reached the crossroads, it was already night. As it was a Sunday, and he had been preaching all day—first in Auburn, then other neighboring communities - Reverend Dinsmore sagged with the weight of his Holiness wagon, which felt much heavier to pull than it had this morning when he'd set out by foot from his home on the outskirts of Auburn. He'd hoped to make it back to his own bed that night, to be able to kiss his wife and grandchildren goodnight, but his pace must've been slow, or he'd lingered too long at his last engagement, for he now knew home, at this point in the night, as an impossibility, and to push onward much longer would be dangerous, because of the bandits he knew lurked these country roads in darkness.

Reverend Dinsmore looked at his watch, which, despite the proper winding he'd given it this morning, and the fact that one proper winding lasted at least a day and a half, had stopped ticking. The hands of the clock stopped at 5:53, hours ago.

The rattling of the wagon's wheels magnified themselves and Reverend Dinsmore concentrated on the wheels' rattle as a source of comfort so as not to strain to hear any other more distant, less comforting noises.

I am a coward, he thought to himself. Why am I such

a coward? The Lord can see the fear in my eyes. All that surrounds me is the peaceful night, the dark unknown as created by our Holy Father. That was the last thing Reverend Dinsmore remembered of that night's walk. A splitting pain in the back of his skull caused the world to go dark.

He awoke to the jouncing of the wagon wheels along a dirt road. Slowly, slowly in the retreating of his mind's fog, he realized he lay inside his own wagon. He could read, backwards, the word "Holiness" stenciled across the white canvas outside of his wagon. He flashed to the memory of his careful stenciling of the word onto the wagon after much deliberation over which word to choose for the wagon's broad side. He'd narrowed the choice to "Holiness" or "Truth", and in the end, he'd decided to stencil "Truth" on the front of the wagon above the handle. "Truth" to guide my way, he'd thought, and "Holiness" to surround me. Now, supine in his wagon, he looked to the wagon's front and saw "Truth" backlit by the morning sun against the white canvas.

Reverend Dinsmore tried to sit up in the wagon, but he couldn't. He discovered himself lashed with rope to the wagon's bed. It was at this point that his up-to-then almost peaceful reverie broke, and a hard, fast panic replaced it.

Who is pulling my wagon? Why am I lashed to my own wagon bed? Who did this to me? What is going on? The Reverend focused his attention to the dull ache in his head, which he hadn't noticed before. His mouth was so dry that he doubted he would be able to cry out. He tried. Barely a croak escaped his lips, surely inaudible against the bouncing wheels over dirt to anyone pulling the wagon, but what if the person pulling the wagon didn't care if Reverend Dinsmore called out, for this person wouldn't do anything to alleviate the Reverend's suffering. The Devil lives to prolong sin, the Reverend thought, and that one fleeting glimmer of the devil in history gave him a small bit of pleasure.

The Reverend Dinsmore soon lost all track of time. A combination of panic and dehydration kept him falling in and out of consciousness; each time he came to, the white canvas of the wagon's top shone with the arcing movements of the sun. At one point, the Reverend felt a strange relief to notice that the sun perfectly fit within the "o" of "Holiness."

He eats one thing—what it is he doesn't know — and his lower left molar disintegrates, and then his teeth shatter. He loses all of his front lower teeth and he spits out shards of teeth like glass with clinks. But this doesn't hurt at all or seem to be terrible. Other people will help him, because he's at a summer camp of some sorts. A girl jumps off a covered bridge, covering her face, trying to commit suicide, which, he thinks, puts his loss of teeth in perspective. To fix his teeth, he has to travel back north with the camp director and two other girl campers. It's a beautiful drive in the back of the director's truck. They ride over a single-track bridge under construction. He's scared, but it seems okay until they go over a flooded area of track. The trailer of the truck detaches and flies out over the water. The girls become very worried, but he remembers to open a window before they sink, and they're easily able to swim to shore, a beachy mud cliff that strikes him as incredibly beautiful.

At some point in the afternoon, the back of the tent nearest the Reverend's head opened and a hand appeared with a cup of water. Another hand raised the back of his head, so as to allow the Reverend a long drink. The tilt of his head combined with his thirst caused much of the water to despairingly cascade down his chin. He did not get the chance to closely examine the hand, but when he thought of this hand, he assumed it must be a man's. But didn't it seem soft? Didn't it cup his head with a certain amount of tenderness? The water, even so little of it, tasted unbelievably good.

Hello! The Reverend called out. Hello out there! Where are we going? Why did you do this to me? Hello? Hello!

But there was no response. The night began to drop again.

To comfort himself, Reverend Dinsmore thought about Truth. He thought about Trees. He thought about Justice and Peace and Retribution. He remembered the dog he had when he was six.

Somewhere amidst these revelries, he realized the wagon had stopped moving. A hand with a knife entered the front of the wagon, splitting open the front flat in between "Tru" and "th". The knife wavered and the Reverend feared it would finally find him, but instead it cut the ropes that bound his feet. After a short time when he could hear footsteps walking around the wagon, the knife again entered the wagon, this time near his head, reaching down to carefully cut the ropes that bound his upper arms.

Reverend Dinsmore had been tied up for so long that he was at first unable to move either his arms or legs, prickles running excruciatingly through his appendages as they struggled to flex themselves. But eventually, he could move, and he struggled to crawl from the wagon. He felt so old. It was indeed night, and the Reverend looked around him. He was in Auburn, in front of his house, which was lit up with a familial warmth. No one else was in sight. His neighbors looked to be home. A dog barked. He could smell dinner from his own house. Slowly, Reverend Dinsmore climbed the front steps of his house. With his hand on the front door, he looked back at the wagon left askew in the yard.

Reverend Dinsmore never used his wagon again. He never preached again. He became a carpenter, his father's work, and he never spoke to anyone of what happened to him. He told his wife he'd gotten lost, and in time, that was the story he himself believed.

PORTRAIT OF ETTA

Here are the beaches of Old Orchard, Rye or Rockaway;
the storm-beaten cliffs of Nantucket, Nahant or
Marblehead; the highlands of Mount Desert, with
the same grand views of the ocean, and covered with
forest trees; the silver clams for which Rhode Island is
famous; freshwater lakes, brooks and the forests
of the White Mountains—thus combining an unlimited
amount of healthful pleasure and enjoyment.
　　—Seguinland Cottage Company Brochure, circa 1915

Etta Luxembourg White was the fourteen-year-old niece of Clarence H. White, founder and chief lecturer of the Seguinland School of Photography, July 6 through August 22, 1917. Etta's parents, Sydney and Claudette White, wanted her to begin her studies at Radcliffe in the fall, but Etta had convinced them that a summer in Seguinland would be the perfect respite before entering life in Cambridge.

The Seguinland Hotel. Five Islands, Maine. Season
opens July 1st, 1917. Jas C. Durrell, proprietor. For one
person in a room the terms are Transient, $3.00 per
day; by the week, $17.50.

Etta had spent her previous fourteen years in central Pennsylvania. Her father, a former set designer in New York. Her mother, a former ballerina, born in Russia to

French parents. Parties of pastry swans. A kitchen of charred sunburnt-orange cast iron pots and pans over varying heats. Six brothers and sisters, of which Etta was the youngest.

Etta wanted to be an architect. Sydney and Claudette wanted her to be able to make a passable to exquisite quiche Lorraine and dance the foxtrot with a Count.

Jas C. Durrell, proprietor of the Seguinland Hotel, greeted Etta White as she entered the lobby of the seaside resort. A cigar.

"Young lady, the esteemed Ms. White, all the way from the outlands of Pennsylvania, am I correct?"

An image on platinum, for Etta, felt like a silver coin she could keep in her pocket. She tried on different styles in the way she tried on books and hats.

Her favorite line from *Middlemarch:* "Here and there a cygnet is reared uneasily among the ducklings in the brown pond and never finds the living stream in fellowship with its own oary-footed kind."

Etta looked at Mr. Durrell. "Our farts are slightly used." She made her escape as Mr. Durrell was left to fumble with the flaming end of his cigar.

~

Clarence H. White lay on the bed of his hotel room in the Seguinland. His wife, Jane, was in the bathroom. Clarence stared at a floating ceiling. And what will you do with Etta, Jane asked. Clarence didn't know what he'd do with Etta. Honestly, she intimidated him. She'd been at his summer photography camp for nearly three weeks. Other children had nicknamed her Prune. Clarence thought a more appropriate nickname would be Nails. He wondered, sometimes, if she might not eat some of the lesser campers, not out of an obscene appetite, but because it would lessen the ignorant stints she would have to endure in her life. Etta, to her uncle, seemed to be in an acerbic time of life usually reached much later—late twenties at least—where meals were as likely to end up on the floor or the wall as the table.

Most of the other campers, Clarence spoke to his wife in the dark afternoon heat, live as if no life were capable of being related without the obligatory childhood trauma; Etta bypasses this like a freight train barreling through a station at which it is not scheduled to stop.

In his hand, Clarence held a photo Etta had taken the week prior, a simple composition, but he could taste the almost muddy, sweet, ripe black fruit of that mulberry bush by the mailbox of his own now distant childhood.

I believe I'll ask her to accompany me this weekend north to Bath, Clarence said, to the government shipyards, and it felt right to him. Yes, that's the thing to do, Jane said as she returned from the bathroom, perfume funneling around her. Encourage the girl.

The shipyards of Bath, a few hours north from

Seguinland, rang with an uncommon clamor. Etta and Clarence worked near each other. The two of us, Clarence said as he squinted against the sun, what a beautiful morning. They ate lunch together, cheese sandwiches and bottles of lemonade, sitting on a railroad tie.

I'm neither pretty nor ugly, Etta said in a lull between ships. My face is neither pleasant nor unpleasant, neither attractive nor unattractive. It's a face one rarely notices. It goes without saying that I wish I was beautiful. That's hardly a confession worth making. But I swear that sometimes I want to be revolutionarily ugly. Perhaps it's because people would at least notice me then.

Men spent themselves. The wooden ribs of a whale cried out to be finished into a hull.

It's hubris, Etta, to think so little of yourself. Do you really think people, including me, aren't sometimes or often or maybe even always dissatisfied with themselves in some way? Do you really think that people, including me, ever really manage to get through life without finding a way to balance their gifts and their pride?

~

"The Skeleton of the Ship"—Bath, Maine, 1917, coated platinum print by Clarence H. White.

"Shelter: Silence & Alchemy"—Bath, Maine, 1917, coated platinum print by Etta L. White.

~

A black quadrangle, ink black and crisp, sifting through the wisp fog, and it all sketched and accented as if with graphite. Jane, you wouldn't believe it, wait until you see. I'll show it to you. An angled ship passing though a white fog dust. She may be the most talented photographer I've seen in ages. I never knew. I've been waiting for this.

Etta White lay on black rocks, the spray of all the oceans upon her. There was a sound, one not in the audible membranes, but through the black planes of waiting. Other noises undoubtedly buzzed and flurried, but it was the waiting to which she listened. It was the waiting to which she ceded.

TEACHING AT NIGHT

My car wouldn't start one night last week after my night class got out. I had to call a tow truck, and ride home with the driver. It was snowing and was supposed to turn to ice in the early hours. The driver said he hadn't felt well that night, but couldn't call out. He worked six p.m. to six a.m. six days a week and lived more than two hours away. I tried to tell myself, the crazy things we do when we're young, as he was probably almost fifteen years younger than me and reminded me of one of my students at the community college who are trying to leave towing and plowing, and get into plumbing or automotive repair.

But the truth is I've never worked that hard, not even when I was twenty-two. As we drove home that night on the interstate, and the snow picked up, I asked him if he ever gets to sleep when he's working. Sometimes, he said, for an hour or so, if I'm lucky, a little catnap. We exited and drove slow up the ramp. He pulled the truck to the side of the road. I thought a strap had come loose on the bed, but he only opened the door and vomited onto the black road, wet clumpy liquid in a pile like someone hurriedly dumped a slushy from 7-11. Sorry, he said and wiped his mouth with his hand, that's the third time tonight. He took a swig of Gatorade.

He dropped off my car at the mechanic, and as my wife sat waiting for me in her car a few feet away to drive me home to bed, I thanked him. Have a good night, he said and extended his hand.

I paused for a split second, not knowing if I wanted to shake, but then I did it anyway, realizing as I did that he'd wrapped his hand in his sweatshirt sleeve.

THE FOLK SONGS OF WASHINGTON COUNTY

I, Edison, am eternally grateful to the Maine Arts Commission for its generosity, and for destroying my life. A Good Idea Grant: $1500 for one project, and I took that money and ran up north into Washington County to collect folk songs from a small band of gypsies that harvested blueberries at the end of summer and lived, supposedly, back off-the-grid somewhere in the woods the rest of the year. My friend, Lazlo, an English professor at Washington County Community College and a folk music aficionado, served as my guide. He was a convincing enough guy to impress the MAC into believing his credentials, and I trusted him, too, maybe more than I should.

He picked me up from the bus station in Bangor in his VW bus. "You're lucky, Edison," he said. "We travellin' in style."

"We will not be sleeping together in the back of this bus," I said, as this was a very important thing to establish from the outset.

"Of course not. I brought a tent. For me."

"Good," I said.

~

Into the back of Lazlo's van, I loaded my machine, a nearly prehistoric conglomeration of brass and steel, pads and nobs, needles and wax cylinders that would record the songs for posterity. I named the machine Father. Why? I could get into that, but why bother, you know? It'll come out eventually. Father weighed a fucking ton and I could barely maneuver him on my own and that's part of the reason I needed Lazlo. But I have to give Father credit: the dude could record music. The most beautiful, deep, rich, soulful shimmerings emerged from the wax cylinders when I played back the recordings. I mean, the shit could go Smithsonian. But I wasn't in it for Museum Fame.

"I have some bad news for you," Lazlo said as we drove and he sneaked a quick glance at me from the driver's seat. "The gypsies are gone."

That's why I was in it. For the gypsy heritage of it. Before my mother died and my father left, they told me I was descended from gypsies, straight out of Romania, and off travelling the world. This was to be a heritage connector trip, or at least that's how I pitched it to the Maine Arts Commission.

"What the fuck you mean they're gone? The gypsies, are you talking about the gypsies?"

"Yeah, they are gypos, you know. That's what they do." Lazlo reached into the center console, digging around for what I presumed was a cigarette. I looked down to follow his groping hand, which was rummaging through a pile of shit that included two bags of potato chips, a tape measure, a few grossly waded up paper towels and, presumably somewhere in there, his cigarettes.

"Don't smoke," I said.

"What, like, now?

"Don't smoke."

"Ever?"

"Ever. Now. In here. You piss me off."

"So I don't get to smoke because I piss you off, is that it?"

"I should just let you rip away—rip those butts!— smoke 'em as fast as you can so your sorry ass'll turn into a spotted penumbra!"

"What the fuck's a spotted penumbra?"

"You're the English professor dude. You tell me."

"Well, I don't know."

"I'm allergic to smoke."

"Since when? You never used to be allergic to smoke. I used to smoke around you all the time. You even smoked yourself, in case you forgot."

"Well, now things have changed. I'm allergic to things. Especially from people who piss me off." I almost felt bad for Lazlo. He'd gone to all this trouble to pick me up in his van, which probably got something like two miles to the gallon, and had agreed to drive me around Washington County for two days in search of folk songs. It was a thing only an ex-boyfriend would agree to. Or an ex-boyfriend who wanted to be a current boyfriend. So...yeah...Lazlo.

"Come on, Edison, don't start the trip like this," Lazlo said, and I could tell he was a little scared of me, which was good. "Besides, all is not lost. I got a back up plan for you."

"You got me a back up plan. How 'bout you just tell me where the gypsies have moved on to and then I can chase them?"

"Because I don't know where they went. And I knew you wouldn't come if they weren't here. So I didn't tell you."

I let that last comment dry like rubber cement on my future. This was, indeed, the story of my pitiful life: I get something almost good, a lead, a break, a grant; then I for some stupid reason rely on other people (often ex-boyfriends) to help me get shit done; and of course those other people inevitably fall short because it's not their life to live, leaving me stranded and pissed and continuing a long line of failings. Sound familiar? You probably know someone like me. I know quite a few someones like me and they all drive me absolutely bat shit crazy, most of all, myself.

"I'm going to take you to the King," Lazlo said, like I was supposed to be excited or something, but I could tell he was even more scared.

"What King? Like fuckin' Elvis or something? This is Washington County, not Graceland. Lazlo, don't fuck with me. We can just turn around and I'll take the next bus back to Portland."

"No, no, no," he said. "You'll like the King. Just you wait. Trust me."

~

I should tell you more about Father. The machine, not the biological progenitor, who's not worth the time anyway. But Father, the machine, is a true thing of antiquated beauty. You know how your grandmother's cast-iron skillet always seems to make better pancakes than any of your new stainless steel wedding presents? That's how Father is. He's been seasoned by eons of grease. He's like your grandma's cast-iron skillet rolled together with her sewing machine, her typewriter and her phonograph. And, on top of that agglomeration, he's better! He's a crank-turning, gear-grinding, toothed anthropological Pegasus! He's got wheels and cogs and wax cylinders, which are the most important because they do the recording of the music, right? I actually don't even know, but honestly, Father is a complicated, persnickety, temperamental soul. I'm still learning how he works, and works best, and I've been tinkering with him for months, ever since I bought his dusty mechanical self at an auction in a barn in Brooks. At the time, I couldn't believe I'd just spent $2000 for, what the auctioneer called, "a rare antique recording machine that looks like it's from The Industrial Revolution, or Mars, and weighs a ton." That was a lot of money for me. In fact, that was indeed the lump sum of my savings, but I'd justified it, as I stood on the chilly auction floor raising my hand as the auctioneer ticked off a mild bidding war, by telling myself it was an investment in my future as a musical anthropologist, which I even knew at the time was bullshit. But then, I got this Good Idea Grant, and I suddenly felt legitimized, like this was the start of a new beginning, like I was leaving behind the long line of wreckage that was my life of waitressing jobs, bad boyfriends, fried food and too much beer. It felt good, better than I'd ever imagined, to take three days off work from the abusive, anger-management cesspool of a restaurant and travel north with Father's bulk wedged below the bus.

My real father was a traveling musician. I guess I shouldn't technically use the past tense when speaking about him, because he could be very much alive, but, you know, if the verb tense fits, use it. He was a kick-ass fiddler, the kind of dude who won awards and grants, not like that really mattered to, or affected, my mother and me. His name was Richard Cohen, but his stage name was The Flaming Dick. Just kidding. That's what my mother and I called him. His real stage name, along with his band, was Ricky Golden and the Klezmer All-Stars. They toured New England.

"So when you gonna admit this is all about your search for your father?" We were camped for the night outside Cherryfield and had just fought about Lazlo setting up his sleeping bag outside. "I mean, come on, you call that antique bag pipe 'Father'. You don't need an English teacher to pick up on that symbolism."

Lazlo was half way out of the van and it was obvious that he meant it as some type of parting shot. Framed in the van's doorway like that, hunched over so I could see his back muscles straining through his sweatshirt, I had to admit Lazlo was a beautiful man, a handsome bear who knew how to spell. I could've done much worse than Lazlo and it would've been nice to have the company in the van on a chilly night, but then I remembered this new-found commitment to my career, to myself as someone who actually finished projects, not just someone who thought up cool projects, but never did them. I didn't need the distraction, even if this particular distraction would've been good insulation.

"First of all," I snapped back, "it's your own fault for bringing that cheap-ass polyester sleeping bag. And"—I was revving up—"it's your fault you're a pussy." I felt a little bad saying that last part, because I knew it wasn't really true, would seem ungrateful and would hurt Lazlo's feelings, but I strode onward in the name of ambition. "And furthermore, of course I know Father is a stand in for my real father! What do you think I am? Stupid?"

And on that last screamed word, I slammed the van door shut on the night. Unforunately for me, and as unbelievable as it may be, I had not completely made the connection between Father and The Flaming Dick, but I'd be damned if I was going to let Lazlo point that out to me and get the upper hand.

The van that night was cold and lonely.

We didn't talk much the next morning. I bought Lazlo a gas station coffee as we drove north, even though he didn't ask for it. Around noon, after we'd had a few hours of chilly silence, Lazlo said that the King was a lighthouse keeper and that we were headed to his lighthouse.

"But we're headed north, inland, away from the coast," I said.

"Yep." I could tell by the way Lazlo said it that he meant, unless you want to really piss me off, you better be quiet and trust me.

I decided I could do that. I could trust him.

~

It turned out Lazlo was right. There was a lighthouse in the middle of Washington County. It was actually on Nicolai (aka "The King") Kundera's farm. He'd had it built site specific, and it sat out there behind his house like a beached beacon whale. It actually looked mighty ridiculous, but what could I say?

"It all comes back to the lighthouses in New England, huh?" Lazlo said as we pulled into the rutted driveway and he hunched over the steering wheel, squinting so that he could fully see the lighthouse in its almost blindingly white glory.

"Have you ever been here before," I asked.

"Yeah, once. Niki had a big contra dance one Saturday night in the bottom of the lighthouse."

"And?"

"Didn't go well. Niki got pissed at everybody for

having heavy feet and rattling the windows of the tower so bad he thought they'd bust."

As we got out of the van, a one-legged chicken 'ran' toward us, if you can call it that. "This better be worth it," I muttered to Lazlo as I fought the urge to kick the one-legged chicken.

"Just wait."

A woman emerged from the farmhouse and stood in the dooryard. It wasn't exactly a greeting. She was about as wide as she was tall, wore a soiled formerly-white apron and exuded an air of don't-fuck-with-me-I've-got-a-pie-in-the-oven.

"Hello, Barta," Lazlo called out rather timidly, I thought. Barta uncrossed her arms and pointed at the lighthouse in a way that communicated, "if you must, you must." Then she went back into the farmhouse. The one-legged chicken hopped after her.

We walk down a path between high grass to get to Nicolai's lighthouse, then we climb the extremely steep stairs from the ground floor to the second floor. It's so small that I have a hard time imaging a contra dance in here not bringing down the whole structure. Nicolai sits in a folding chair. Before I can even say hello, Lazlo has whipped out a pair of cigarettes, Nicolai reaches, Lazlo lights and they're smoking together so fast I feel like a bit of a prude.

As he exhales, Lazlo says, "she doesn't smoke." Nicolai shrugs as if to say, too bad, what do I care? Nicolai is toothless, very small, and wears faded overalls with a fuzzy red wool cap that I bet never leaves his head. He's so skinny his overalls look like he tied a denim garbage bag around his waist, but forgot to cinch it tight. He coughs often and I imagine some organ inside him will soon fly from his mouth. Lazlo whispers to me that he has a bum lung.

Without warning, Lazlo and Nicolai start talking in some kind of foreign language I've never heard before, some kind of guttural timpani. I don't even know Lazlo speaks this language. I'm impressed. For a few moments, they talk, Lazlo clearly regarding the old man with deference. I'm actually relieved to be left out of the conversation, as it gives me a moment to take in my surroundings. The room's only about fifteen feet in diameter and has a huge brass-plated and glass light that takes up the majority of the space.

Suddenly Nicolai is speaking to me: "You like my lighthouse?" I tell him I do, very much. "I had it built in Romany style," he says, looking sideways at Lazlo to see if I get the joke. I laugh like an imbecile, pronouncing each word—ha. ha. ha.—to make sure Nicolai knows I get it. He looks pleased that I like his joke.

Lazlo says, "Edison came here to sort out her father issues." I glare at him, and for an instant, I consider calling Lazlo a fucker, but I can't really do that now in front of Nicolai, and Lazlo knows that. I owe him one. But to my surprise, Nicolai doesn't respond, only smiles and shrugs, like what do I care. I wonder if he's even understood what Lazlo said.

"You want chicken legs?" Nicolai asks in a practiced way, and from somewhere, I don't know where, he pulls out a plastic plate of some kind of deep-fried sticks. "My specialty," he says and smiles, that is if you can smile without teeth. The image of the one-legged chicken immediately comes to mind, but before I can do anything to resist, Lazlo is biting into one of them, and I know I don't have a choice.

They're crunchy, and taste like, of course, chicken.

There's an awkward silence as we chew and Nicolai smiles without eating. For a minute, I think he's saving all the chicken legs for us, which seems sweet, then I realize there's no way he could eat one of these crunchy sticks without teeth.

Suddenly, and much faster than I'd expect, Nicolai jumps up and flashes the huge light directly at his farmhouse. "That's our cue," Lazlo says to me. I don't understand. "Time to go get Father," he says and heads down the stairs for the van.

By the time we haul Father's metal bulk up to the top of the lighthouse, Barta is already up there, a guitar cradled in her lap. In this light, which almost seems holy, her skin is the pallor of garlic cloves. She also has a mason jar of whiskey, which she sips and passes.

I set up Father and now, with his bulk, the room is very tight. Nicolai and Barta eye the machine that will suck the songs out of their bodies with some suspicion, but they don't say anything against it. I feel a little like a grave robber.

They start to play, and I record.

Nicolai's fingers, that only a few moments ago looked like gold-ringed sausages, now dance over his violin strings, unspeakably light, scampering up and down the melody. Barta, by contrast, doesn't know how to play the guitar, but she sure knows how to beat it to near death, which really does look imminent for her guitar, possibly the most beat-up, cracked thing I've ever seen, the neck held together by an old guitar string and not a fret in sight. I remember thinking it definitely came out of a dumpster. She hits that poor thing like she's beating a rug hanging out on a clothesline, no chord changes, simply a rhythmic beating so savage it's, in comparison with Nicolai's ribaldly skillful fiddle, beauty and the beast.

Honestly, after a few minutes, I don't know how long I can actually stand this music. Lazlo, on the other hand, leans back in his chair, closes his eyes and sips his whiskey, obviously ready to let the ages roll by. Even with my visceral discomfort, I can also feel the music's transcendent quality. If one gets over the fact that an instrument is meeting its violent end, there's also a carnal root stirring that signifies this music is from some deep source, long ago, and that it's beyond the bounds of my admittedly poor pop-music sensibilities. This is soul music, my family's music. Welcome home, Edison, my mothers say. We've been waiting so long for you to find us.

There's this blissed out moment where I'm

uncomfortable and I'm watching myself be uncomfortable and it feels good, warm and tingly. Then, in a moment, it all falls apart.

~

Sometimes I wonder, how the hell did I get myself into this? Why did I leave my entire life in Portland? But I did it and it was, honestly, easy. Now, around these parts, I'm known as the Queen. When I think back to those moments, those days, in which I became the Queen, despite my own disbelief and resistance, I think of rupture, and all the ways things burst. I think of blood, grist, all the violence of change as an act of aggression against the self. Mainly I think of Nicolai. The doctors said his lung burst, or at least I think that's what they said. Is that even possible? Can you bust a lung? All of a sudden, as he played that afternoon, as he looked so happy, he began to vomit blood. There was no time for anything else. He died within the hour. It takes a lot of time and effort, an inordinate amount of scrubbing, to remove blood from wood. Maybe Nicolai had special blood. Some of it seeped through the cracks of the lighthouse's second floor, patterned and pooled on the floor below to create a much smaller version of death. The blood made an image of a lung. There's so much space inside a lung, so spacious and hollow.

My own lungs work right now, crinkling up to exhale, filling up in a stretch expansion on the inhale.

As I sit on the second floor of the lighthouse, Father behind me, I breathe and look out the light. Barta is gone.

When I play Father back, it's the teeth grinding in the cylinders that release the sound of joy.

Lazlo says he'd like to come visit me, the Queen, but I say no, not now. I'm collecting myself. I like it that way.

DR. WHITE

She showed me the book because she thought I'd be interested; it contained some partial discussions of a French philosopher and linguist whose work on form, font and serif we both fancied, though I most liked the way the French philosopher's name was spelled and had only read a grand total of two paragraphs of her work. But they were good paragraphs. The book was called *Curatorial Studies in the Modern Museum* and she'd acquired it at Yes Books, the enigmatically optimistic used bookstore on Commercial Street. Pascha, the rare book dealer, had given it to her with his characteristic taciturnity, grunting, "lady," before returning behind his stacks of un-inventoried acquisitions, which more than likely only served as a barrier between the hermetic, bearded book dealer and the world, and would probably never diminish. I neglected to spend much time with the book, though I remember an accumulation of pages with a pleasing palette of white and tan and gray, an agglomeration that lacked the ability to offend yet still possessed the faintly sinister odor of expensive perfume worn by those who frequented gallery openings during The Festival of What Was Not Eternal and whose eyes remained far too closed towards what they looked.

The palette reminded me of a conversation I'd had with Dr. White, a cardiologist from Maine Medical, when we'd found each other at the record player of a friend's apartment. It had been a Sunday afternoon party in January. A quiet desperation, punctuated with dirty snow piled five feet high beneath street lamps, hovered outside the apartment and tried to thrust its polished skull into the party whenever someone opened the front door. But the party itself was warm and cozy, bolstered by meat quiche, mulled wine, candles and Dr. White's musical selections, for he'd assumed the role of disc jockey though it wasn't his party, he didn't know most of the records in the collection, and he admitted ceasing to pay attention to music fifteen years ago. Dr. White chose the records he played by heft and album cover; the heavier the record the more fitting he reckoned it'd be for a winter Sunday; and the more wintery colors an album cover exhibited, the more likely he'd play it. He'd just set the needle into a record called "Elan" by Good Winter, an easy choice according to his criteria, and the ambient music reinforced this. Dr. White, who shared my interest for philosophy without enjoying the reading of it, leaned over and told me the following anecdote which I've condensed, for better or for worse:

> *A certain philosopher saw a top. He pursued the top, which was very tall, but the snow was heavy and he was tired. The top made a long flat black ribbon across the snow. At the edge of the property, a birdhouse with a white hat. Beyond, the drab hills, among them, bears. And the top, followed by the philosopher, moving towards them all.*

I related this story, quite inadequately (for how does one relate the presence of the top?) to the woman with the Curatorial Studies book. Did she appreciate it? I couldn't tell, but her mouth moved and she checked her phone, which was new and white. She said she'd thrown her back out shoveling two days ago. Strange, I said, and be careful because Dr. White also told me he was busiest as a surgeon in winter, for that's when people's hearts most failed, heart attacks when shoveling, despondency and other such illnesses.

The Owl in the Road

I placed the tines of the fork against the edge of the plate and finished my beer. There had been a few stray snowflakes against the air when I'd entered the restaurant at the onset of evening, but now as I exited, it was only cold.

A month ago, I'd moved into an attic apartment in the Old Port and upon leaving the restaurant, I walked in that direction. The restaurant, named after a James Baldwin character, was a new marble and brass addition to my life. Usually I spent most of the day in the Historical Society, Longfellow's family home, a poet of whom I didn't know a single poem.

This was all during a phase of my life I call my Historical Period, and when I do so, I roll my eyes. I'd decided at this juncture of early middle age that I wanted to write history books. I did not concern myself with what I then thought a mute point—I never read history books. Why didn't this discrepancy strike me as odd, if not foreboding certain doom? I don't honestly know. I wish I did. But I was young enough, bold enough and ignorant enough to think that if I set my sights toward the venerable hills of history, immersed myself within them, then I would emerge from this inundation with a book clutched to my breast, my own book, with my name emblazoned across the spine. Perhaps there would be lectures to give, tours throughout the regional historical societies and important questions posed by earnest men in tweed and beautiful, serious women with bobs.

I even came up with a few select theories on history and how I would write it. I wanted to be consumed by the questions and absolved by my search for their answers. We historians—the first person plural felt boldly inclusive to me—do not revel in imprecision, as seems possible in other (read: 'lesser') disciplines, like fiction or drama or poetry, where the suspension of the unknown provides fodder for inspiration. No, instead, we want to know exactly what happened. "History, of course, is an interpretative art..." I could hear myself say this, surprisingly without irony, in response to a question during some talk. "At least in so far as the books are concerned, but events happen in singularity. One thing happens, then it's forgotten." I wanted to be someone who remembered. And yes, the slippage of memory held its own appeal to me. As I look back on this appeal, its mist and shroud, I cringe more than a little. I've forgotten so many things. And yet, there I was—a young historian interested in Collective Memory, indeed, obsessed with it. How does a population remember, and how do we forget? The ribboning obscurities, theoretical and blossoming, made me ripple with pleasure. I now know otherwise. I was so good at fooling myself. But to return to history, my history, I had a book I wanted to write. *The Life and Mysterious Death of Private Hiram T. Smith: The Only*

Casualty of the Bloodless Aroostook War. Of course I'd come up with the title first, and I thought once I had that, the rest would just roll out of my pen and before I knew it, the book would be in print.

I found myself obsessed with the topic after I'd attended a talk by the venerable historian Earl Shettleworth entitled: "The County: A Photographic History". In this talk, Earl mentioned the Aroostook War, a bloodless 'war', more of an escalation without battle, over the Canadian border along Aroostook County. I think it had the most to do with logging rights. Something like that. I remember Earl mentioning Hiram T. Smith as the only casualty, and a slightly mysterious one at that, of this bloodless war. The paradox intrigued me, in fact enough so that I moved to Portland, rented a studio for way too much money in the Old Port, got myself a membership to the Historical Society and vowed to end this little experiment with a book of history for my troubles, a book that could change my (let's be honest here) up-until-then quite miserable life.

I'd moved from Halifax where I'd become something of a legend, more infamous, for a certain evening of poetry readings over which I presided. I told myself that, in Halifax, I tried to harness the energy of youth and then provide an outlet for that energy, but…but… well, before I get to that particular sordid detail of my past, let me say that I unequivocally succeeded in my attempt to harness the youthful energy of Poetry. I packed that poor little coffee shop every Wednesday night. They sold more caramel non-fat, double red-eyes during our poetry slam than they did the entire week. We had people lining the walls and poets had to arrive within the first fifteen minutes to get a slot, or they'd be doomed to sit and sulk in the audience with their blueberry muffin atop their folded manuscript. Big Poet's Bus was written up numerous times in The Coast and The Chronicle Herald as a positive youth outlet, or some other shit, and we even got a few pieces on television. The station called me up: "Hey, Red, can you give us a quote—what does Poetry mean to the People?" And I told them, or at least I gave them some mouthful of words that I now forget, but that at the time I thought good, actually quite inspired. And so the Big Poet's Bus rolled on, Wednesday nights, slamming down the vowels, sucking in the syllables and I was the man behind the table, smiling and talking and shaking my finger, until…oh, it all happened so fast.

As one of the perks of founding and continually organizing the clusterfuck that Big Poet's Bus became, I would periodically, not even regularly, hyper-sporadically really, schedule myself as the Featured Poet of the night. In other words, the peons and slumgullions had from 6:30 to 8:00 to do their stuff, prance their ponies, insult each other, praise their grandmothers, whatever they wanted. But then at 8:00, and promptly on the hour, mind you (there's only so much of that shit a man can stand), I cut them off and it was time to listen to the Featured Poet. Sometimes I brought them in from as far away as New Jersey, and always volunteer, plus a cut of the door, which was usually spent easily on beer afterwards. It always surprised me to what lengths these men would travel for an audience. Honestly, that was a thing—the Featured Poets were almost always men. That's just the way it worked out—what can I say? I didn't necessarily want it that way, but honestly, that's who I found on the circuit, or at least that's what I told myself at the time. And I wasn't mistaken, or not really. Maybe I was. I don't know, I don't know... maybe I knew, but didn't really want to. Maybe I was a closet misogynist who hated every woman's bones with a subconscious fury, which I was eventually accused of, but I don't think so. Maybe I disliked a few people, Svetlana among select others, but it was far from hate, more of a malaise like egg wash.

So there I was, 8:00 on my own Featured Poet night, after I'd prepared and practiced my poems for three days. I watched my watch turn the hour and I headed toward the stage to cut off the open reading and begin my own. All of a sudden, a young woman jumped on stage, not more than twenty-five years old, and started yelling, "I'm the Featured Poet! I'm the Featured Poet! I'm the Featured Penis! Where are the Women in this thing? I am the Featured Pussy!" Oh boy, and what was worse—the audience even liked this pussy riot girl, even though she was not performing at all other than shouting and hopping around on stage like a pink chimp. I gave her a moment—her moment of fame—

then I decided I'd had enough. An hour and a half of terrible poetry can do twisted things to a mind and I was more than ready to do my own terrible poetry. So I went on stage. Maybe it was the blood rush of the stage, the burn of the lights, the eyes of the audience, something... but my mind went blank. The young woman did not want to peacefully leave the stage, so I pushed her. Quite hard, actually. This was, retrospectively, a real mistake, but in the moment, I simply acted off my blank mind. The young woman—she was sort of a waif—flew off stage, fell and hit her head against an amp. Nothing more than a minor cut. But, I admit, it looked bad, very bad. After that moment, chaos reigned down upon my life, far beyond that moment. I was arrested for assault, spent three days in jail, but not before I had slices of pizza, bottles of beer, cookies, lattes, quarters and whatever else was at hand thrown at me. They really hurt. The rapid arrival of the police was actually a relief, for as they cuffed and stuffed me, they protected me from more serious harm. And that, in a prolonged moment of various and unwanted apologies, was the end of my life in Halifax.

I surrendered Big Poet's Bus to other less volatile, younger hands; I surrendered custody of my fourteen-year-old daughter to Svetlana; I surrendered my job, cashed in my savings and surrendered myself to universal loss. I moved to the attic studio in the Old Port, and I began to assemble a historian's toolbox. Why? Because it felt right. And I had nothing better to do.

As is often the case with titanic meltdowns, it was all actually a relief. The thought of never hearing another installment of Big Poet's Bus brought such catharsis that I wanted to squeal, however some of the other things left behind (mainly my daughter Roxanna) did not thrill me. As the scandal emerged, Svetlana took the opportunity to inform me that she could sue for sole custody and get it, plus much more. But this is not a story about them. No, let me return my wandering mind to where it started—my walk from Sonny's back to my studio on Silver Street.

It is not surprising, in retrospect, that I became obsessed with being a historian, with the writing of History, and generally with remembrance, because everyone in my former life was in the process, some quite quickly and vehemently, of forgetting me. Goodbye, Red, good riddance. I so desperately wanted to be remembered, if not by my family and friends, then by History, an entity much larger and more forgiving, one that will be around much longer.

My boot heels clicked off the bricks, my hands thrust into my pockets, and the night took me in and asked me questions, practical questions I wanted answered. How would I write this book? How does one write such things? My afternoons in the Historical Society Library were enjoyable, but mainly for the presence of its beautiful books, like being in a bookish womb, but I had been going there for the past month and, although I kept sending the librarians off into the shelves for this book or that book and I took copious notes (things like, "good book, this one! Important fact!"), I really did not make any significant progress. In actuality, I felt more like history's equivalent of a thumb twiddler.

However, even though I didn't do much work, at least I had moved past my less than propitious entry into the Historical Society culture, which is worth its own quick digression.

On my first day as a member of the Historical Society, a sixty-plus year old assistant librarian with a beautifully elaborate, silvered handlebar mustache encouraged me to "take a look around." I was wandering through the, I now know, off-limits balcony area, absently searching for some random book I'd looked up in the card catalogue when I sharply heard, "What are you doing up there?!" The head librarian, a woman a few years younger than me but decidedly tougher looking in a librarian sort of way, was standing on the ground floor, pointing an accusingly stubby finger at me. All shuffled background noise in the library suddenly ceased. "Are you looking for a book?!" I said, far too half-heartedly, that I was. "Are you a member?!" Yes. "Well you can't be up there. We have to get the books for you." Oh. "What's the call number of the book you're looking for?" 641? The head librarian turned to the sheepish-looking assistant librarian and said, "He's in the wrong place. Come back down and we'll get it for you. And don't ever go up there again!" I quickly retreated to the first floor where I began sweating profusely, red-cheeked, and I was convinced that everyone in the library could smell my embarrassed body odor.

I fled into the bathroom to avoid the further flushing of my face. I peed and pressed the handle to flush the toilet, but nothing happened. I pressed the handle down again, held it a little longer and then, to my horror, I watched the water level in the bowl steadily and alarmingly rise until it reached the rim. Despite my pleading protests, the water spilled over and began to slowly cascade down the side of the porcelain and across the black tile floor. This slow spill was a sensation like no other. That moment when the water flowed down the bowl and began to pool across the floor was the equivalent of a psychotic break. All the material, and liquid, that should've normally been contained so neatly had gotten loose and was in the process of ruining everything. The vision that stuck in my head was one of permanent and perpetual vomiting. And there was nothing, absolutely nothing I could do to stop the misfortune. I fell back into a panicked dance on my tip toes and began to spin my head around like there was some thing I could spot that would stop the event. I checked the door to make sure it was locked; it wasn't and I hastily locked it. Then I peered into the bowl and discovered one solitary floating turd about the size of a tater tot. Suddenly it all came clear to me. I had done nothing to clog the toilet; I was a victim of plumbing misfortune. Whoever had last used the bathroom left me this floating dilemma. But what should I do now? I didn't know.

The water lever remained perilously close to the rim and showed no signs of decline. I threw a wad of paper towels onto the puddle and considered what the conversation would be like with the head librarian as I attempted to clarify that, while the toilet was now clogged and overflowing, I was not guilty of the clog, that I was not trying to pull a "clog and run." None of the possibilities for this conversation seemed good to me. I noticed that the water level had finally fallen a quarter of an inch, and so I grabbed the black rubber industrial plunger from the corner of the room and slowly placed it in the bowl. Displaced water, in angry mouthfuls, slipped over the rim and around my boots, but this seepage seemed a mere inconvenience if the effort succeeded. Two quick plunges and I cleared the toilet. I hastily scooted around some paper towels with my foot in a pitiful attempt to soak up the remaining water. Good enough, I said to myself, and unlocked the door. The historical society library was bustling with lots of serious people who had no idea that their bathroom was not pleasant. No one had been waiting for the bathroom, thank god, and I quickly left the library without so much as glancing at the head librarian.

One would've thought I'd have taken the hint after such an inauspicious beginning and given up, but no, history called me and I was determined to answer. I'd read somewhere during my history feeding frenzy—or perhaps it was an original thought, but I sincerely doubt it—that history is a work in progress, a constant writing and rewriting as opposed to museum-quality sculpture in milk-white marble. Well, that very well might be, and in fact such ambiguous philosophical statements are what drew me originally to want to write history, but I was still left with a very tangible problem, one that increasingly stared me in the face the longer I sat at one of the long green-reading-lamp-illuminated tables in the Historical Society: the Aroostook War was boring and the life and death of Private Hiram T. Smith was boring, too. It had already been written, if only lightly but with a decidedly marbled tone, because it was so boring. Some old Maine coon cat of a historian had already realized this and only devoted a few pages here and there to the phenomenon. At first I thought this was a good sign, as it pointed out to me a hole in the scholarship that I'd gladly fill, but then I began to realize the reason for the gap. It punched me in my historical gut, and it was this simultaneously winded and bloated feeling that accompanied me home from Sonny's that evening. I took a circuitous route, trying to lose myself in the tangle of streets that couldn't have been more than a half mile square, but yet, especially at night, felt like miles of myopic brick.

I must've been passing a café or some type of kiosk when my eyes wandered to a flyer: Port Veritas Poetry Slam. Here in Portland. The date was the following evening. I snorted like one who'd lost his faith, and walked on, telling myself I was blessedly now a Writer of History who no more had to meddle with the posing egos of slam poetry. Good riddance. God, it felt good. I eventually arrived at my building, the bottom floor a strange hookah bar that always had a trickle of customers no matter what time of night I returned home. I thought of ember fires burning cindery as I walked by the window and climbed the four flights of stairs to my little room. I fell into the unmade bed. Hello, Herodotus, History is not the land of Milk and Honey I thought it was, more a melancholy tract littered with clogged toilets, blank faces and dead stories. It was much later than I'd thought, my night walk lasting longer than expected and I fell asleep on my bed.

In my sleep, I dreamt of smoke that was at first amorphous and omnipresent, harmless and light. I couldn't see anything and I pawed at the swirling wall before me. It felt like my hands were claws that, no matter how sharp, passed without catching through the smoke. At some point in the dream, I thought the smoke was from the infernal hookah bar and I'd convinced myself that I could sniff apples or something else one might mix with tobacco and stuff into a pipe. All this annoyed the shit out of me and I bucked against consciousness to exit sleep. If I was going to dream, I wanted an interesting (i.e., pleasing) dream, not one addled with carcinogenics. But the dream, as they often do, had something else in mind. Without warning, the smoke changed, somehow altered its substance, and became sooted cinder tinted with flame red rims and now I could undeniably smell something more substantial burning, a forest fire, I thought, or a house fire—whatever the fire morphed into was serious and I began to sweat. The dream oxygen aired itself out and I could feel my ability to breath rapidly diminishing. The fire was fully ready to take me, but I did not want this to happen. I fought as the fire choked me, and suddenly I knew my life was in danger, real palpable danger, the kind of panic state that threatened to sieve me into ash and sand. Then a hand was on my shoulder, turning me around and around, spinning me, some disembodied hand. I looked down at the hand resting on my shoulder and I somehow recognized it as the girl's hand who I'd shoved off stage in Halifax. Hello? Hello, I shouted. No answer. Smoke grew thicker. Breath shrank into knots, a castle's battlements emptied themselves upon me. The hand on my shoulder was now a claw whose grip was vice-like. I felt myself shrinking away at an alarming pace. Daddy! I heard my daughter Roxanna's voice scream at me. Daddy, it's the Tongue of Fire. The Tongue of Fire, Daddy!

And with that I shot bolt upright in the bed, finally awake and covered in sweat, gasping, half expecting to see the entire studio engulfed in a four-alarm fire from which there could be no escape. But no, there was no fire. The room was only quiet and dark. Four-thirty in the morning. I was so fully awake that, if I was a runner, I could've gone for a three-mile run, but I was far from a runner, so instead I made a cup of coffee. The bitter darkness hit me in my sleeping soul and felt so good, helping me to leave the dream back in bed. For despite the fact that I'd made it out of the dream, it felt like I'd paid quite the price for this, like I'd just killed a man for easy money and ran, ran, ran. It wasn't so uncommon for me to experience dream hangovers, but this one had its own special crushing force, a visceral ephemera like the dream had carelessly torn a sheaf of paper from my soul, leaving a jagged edge that had given me a wicked paper cut, one that would not lessen its sting not matter the salve. In short, despite my discomfort and raw nerves, I felt alive, more alive than I had in months, able to finally feel the jangling nerves throughout my body.

Now it was 4:45. I'd just had my first cup of coffee, headed inexplicably and perhaps foolishly towards my second. The Historical Society didn't open for almost six hours. What would I do with myself? What could I do indeed? The city was still a jumbled arrangement of sleeping stone, the kind that discouraged wakefulness, but I didn't care. I was awake, oh was I ever awake, more awake than I'd been for weeks, months, years. I could feel the dark of predawn goading me: "Come on, Red, you wimp! Do it! Do it, old boy!" Do what? I didn't know what the darkness had awakened in me. Then I heard Roxanna's voice again from the dream a few moments ago, crystal clear as if she was in the room with me. The Tongue of Fire? I drew another blank. What did it mean, any of it? I was confused as coal, as only someone can be who relies far too heavily on the most precarious of inadequacies, the written word.

I threw open the window, expecting to hear a far off seagull pilfering fish from the wharves and to feel the rush of a bracing night, but instead something else flew in through the window, fluttering and diffuse, a tired, obnoxious thing, red and ruffled and breathing hard, a slivered muscle. I recognized it as a tongue, and not something that I particularly wanted to see, but there it was. What could I do—I'd opened the window, I'd let her in. She lay quivering in a blood red stoop as if she had traveled a very long way to get here, or perhaps she was (I almost wrote it, then took it back, and now finally have decided to indeed write it) coming home. It was undeniable. This poor, dirty thing sitting on the floor of my apartment definitely felt like it belonged to me, as a long-lost child, or one's amputated toe suddenly appearing on someone's foot lying on a beach. I had the urge to immediately swoop up the sagging bundle, pretend I'd never seen her, and throw her back out into the night—"sorry little tongue poem, not for you, little vowel sounds, go ahead, fly on, flap yourself!" Lord knows that was my first instinct, and maybe I should've heeded it. I wouldn't have told anyone about it and indeed I would've blocked it from my memory, compartmentalized that little sucker in a locked box vault somewhere in the lower intestines of my memory. But then again, I also knew if I did this questionable act of forced forgetting that the memory would return, come back up one day like regurgitated bile, and in a far less attractive form than was currently presented before me. In short, my conscience took over and I knew what I had to do. Once I surrendered to this inevitability, I immediately felt sleepy, much sleepier than I remembered being, for it was still five in the morning and I am not normally that early of a riser. And so, despite the disturbing dream, the poetic visitation through the window, and most significantly the cup of coffee, I fell back into a deep sleep, the kind of muffled release that only comes from the sensation of something indomitably large, heavy, and thus comforting, pressing down against one's limp form.

I'm tempted to resist the urge to tell you this second dream, for fear of diffusing the former's power, but the second dream was so simple that it will only take a moment. I was driving in a car at night—both of these are already disheartening to me for I try very hard to never drive a car, let alone drive a car at night, and yet there I was doing both, quite poorly I might add and with an increasing panic. The headlights illuminated two strips of halogened road. I drove hands clenched to wheel. Then an owl alighted at the edge of my headlights, a large barn owl, I think, who turned its wizened head to stare into the oncoming beams. No time to think, boom, I ran it over, and I didn't hear or feel a thing. That was that and the dream ended. No feelings accompanied this event. It simply happened like the clap of a hand, and then I was awake. It was mid afternoon. How had I slept so long? I never sleep that long. I was surprised my body even allowed it. I soon discovered I was rabidly hungry and I devoured a bowl of Cheerios. Was the milk slightly rotten? Who cares. I had another bowl and took a shower. I dressed and picked up the poem that had flown in through my window the previous evening. She had cleaned herself up quite a bit since I last observed her up close. Small line edits, a few altered punctuation points, justified margins, and she looked good, but fundamentally she was still the same rolling red muscle I'd found last night. I put the thrumming thing into my pocket and headed out, past the hookah bar whose smoke now almost, but not quite, enticed me to enter. Would I do so one day?

The Port Veritas Poetry Slam took place in a small bar, low ceiling, good beer, cash only. It was already crowded when I arrived, but there were still a few sign-up slots open. I ordered a beer, clean and bitter, like a peeping frog. Then someone called my name from stage. I hadn't heard it pronounced that way for a long time, the way the syllables cascaded together like poured water. I approached the stage, and stepped up onto it. The Lights and the Rarest of Attentions. I cleared my throat, reached into my pocket and extracted the tongue. She shuddered with nerves and power. She knew so much more than me, and I put her in my mouth, leaning toward the microphone. Familiar words and images, their voices, came up and flew through me, distinct and presaged, horned, great and hooting forth, from the lowest registers of my being where they'd habitually dwelt in obscurity and perfumed doubt. But no longer—now they were free.

Battery Steele, Peaks Island

It's always autumn when I think of it, the foghorn at regular intervals, and we're walking across a series of hand-nailed planks that form a haphazard boardwalk to the backshore of the island.

It had been raining all day, steady though not hard, vacillating between mist and varied droplets for hours. The sea was a slate gray-green and the surf spit white spray along the line of breakers.

Turning back towards the Battery, the birch trunks drew thin white lines across a crimson and orange canvas, poles put in at angles to distribute the weight of color and break up its walled overwhelm.

Empty cement turrets riddled with weeds looked out to Junk of Pork and the open ocean where, it's rumored, two German soldiers washed ashore during World War II. They were buried clandestinely; I often wonder where their graves are.

We all sat in a circle for the planning meeting in the field behind the Battery. For the art festival that took over the Battery every fall, I wanted to dress as a Mailman and distribute letters during the procession from the landing to the Battery. As our group of volunteers walked beneath the southern turret on our way back to the ferry, she came up to me and said she liked my idea, which was such a relief because I wasn't even sure if I liked my idea. I can't remember what else we talked about that afternoon in October, but six years later we married and I still write her letters.

THE NIGHT RIDES OF JIMMY DEMILLO

for Kevin Sweeney

T hey always had it out for Jimmy DeMillo. Maybe it was because his uncle owned the big restaurant on the mainland. But I think it was something else. Something there is that hates a rebel, and that hate brings out a mean streak in people who feel utterly justified, even vindicated, in ridding the world of rebels like Jimmy DeMillo. Maybe such people rationalized their hate by saying that they were protecting their innocent daughters, their little kids.

But I was a kid and I didn't hate Jimmy DeMillo. In fact, I loved Jimmy in the way only a six-year old boy can love a twenty-one year old high school dropout. Jimmy wasn't a bad kid, or maybe he was. I didn't know. All I knew was that Jimmy loved to ride his motorcycle around the island. Some Saturday nights he'd do it for hours in his white undershirt, jeans and black boots on a summer evening, his hands perched up high on his handlebars like a speeding king on his throne. He never wore a helmet and he rode fast. That's what I think Jimmy loved most: the speed.

There were a few Saturday evenings when my parents would let me play outside after dinner, letting slip my usual bedtime. No worry of homework or getting up for school, just the slowly fading summer light on the island full of people who loved it like we did. On the nights I remember, Jimmy was out riding and when I heard the growl of his bike coming close to our little yard, I ran to the gate. A handful of times he'd nod to me as he sped by, never a wave or a smile, just a tight quick nod, but it was enough, years later as I remember, to give me a quick cut of happiness. Jimmy saw me. Me and Jimmy, together. My man, Jimmy DeMillo.

I heard about the accident from my father who was the island doctor, though Jimmy's injuries had been too severe for my father to help him and Jimmy had to be rushed by medic boat to the mainland. It had been a Saturday evening fallen into night and Jimmy had been out riding. It was a long thin pipe that did it, my father said, laid out at a turn in the road like a sleeping snake where it would've been nearly impossible for Jimmy to see it, especially at the speed he took the turns on the back side of the island. I asked my father if Jimmy was dead. He said he didn't know. Head injuries were dangerous things, he said, you never knew for sure their extent, and of course Jimmy wasn't wearing a helmet.

It was another Saturday, but now at the end of summer when the nights came down early and the air already held a chill, when I heard the growl of a motorcycle again in the distance. It can't be, I thought to myself, and I rushed out of the house, despite my father's protests, and out into the dark where I stood by the gate. I saw the pinpoint of the headlight first, and I immediately knew it was Jimmy. But as he got closer, I could tell something was different, something was wrong. I noticed what I thought was a white mass hovering around his head. An instant later and Jimmy roared by, riding faster than ever, and a chill swept through my body. I wanted to cry out, but I couldn't. The white mass I'd seen was Jimmy's head wrapped in bandages so that it became impossible not to picture him as some kind of mummy. His face, for that split instant as he sped by, had been set in a hollow-eyed snarl, his skin slashed with wounds. I hardly recognized him, as his former swagger and confidence were gone, and in their place resided something I could only describe as determined misery, anger, and undoubtedly, revenge. I ran back inside to the safety and warmth of our house. My father, looking up from the evening paper in his reading chair, said, "that wasn't Jimmy DeMillo, was it?" I couldn't answer him, because I didn't know.

I wasn't the only person that night to see Jimmy. The next day the fear rippled through the island, and the rumors raged from the ferry landing through the café and the Cock-Eyed Gull. Jimmy had gone too far, they said. Even my young ears could tell that was the sentiment. But me, I felt like I'd lost an older brother, or he'd turned to some dark side and no longer acknowledged me.

I never found out if Jimmy found out who put that pipe out in the road. I never knew if he got his revenge. The next evening I kept my attention turned to our front windows in case I heard the distant roar of a motorcycle. I still hoped it would be Jimmy, the Jimmy of old in his jeans and his white shirt, and in my dreams, he'd not only nod, he'd wave, sometimes he'd even smile at me, his good friend, his little brother. I never heard a motorcycle that evening and I lay in my bed that night, still listening for the sound. All noises that drifted into my open window that night were Jimmy. I couldn't fall asleep for hours. Eventually I slept. In the middle of the night I was startled from sleep by a distant sound. I lay in my bed listening. As it grew louder, I realized it was the sound of a siren, and not just one siren, but a bevy of them, what sounded like dozens of wailing sirens circling the island.

Somehow I fell back to sleep. It wasn't so hard, as I must've been exhausted after staying up to listen so late. The next day, I asked my father why there'd been so many sirens the night before. He put down his paper, folded it up, in such a way that I knew he meant to tell me something important. It was Jimmy, he said, I know you liked him.

I never found out what Jimmy did, but I feel like I don't have to. I know. Whatever it was, the island police were too scared to handle Jimmy on their own and they called in back up from the mainland. And they all went after Jimmy that night. They chased him around the island, and Jimmy fled on his bike. It was the kind of high-speed chase that never happened on the island. They chased him, my father said, around the edges and into the middle where much of it was dense forest. My father paused, and coughed, looking down at his folded newspaper. Did they catch him, I yelled, did they kill Jimmy? No, he said, they didn't catch him. Jimmy disappeared into the interior of the island. No one knows where he is, but they're waiting for him.

Out Past Matinicus

My Captain does not answer, his lips are pale and still;
My father does not feel my arm, he has no pulse nor will;
 —Walt Whitman

The Captain's name seemed to define itself the instant I heard it uttered. Like the raised letters of a sail maker's sign, it secured itself singularly in a small corner of my mind where it stayed contained, prescribed and authoritative.

As Ms. Palatine explained who the Captain was, referring at length to a number of his voyages, I recognized the name of a distant sea over which I'd once crossed in a tremendous storm, a journey that cost me many lives, and then I recognized the name of an obscure sea in which I'd been shipwrecked and left floating for dead, and so too another sea that claimed my brother's life one October. As Ms. Palatine prefaced the Captain's entrance, I felt as if his life lay over top of mine like a blanket, the names of his experiences surrounding and overshadowing my own.

Beneath the Captain's grizzled sea beard, when it was finally presented to me, I saw the face of my own beloved seas. He'd known what I'd known and more. I trembled before the complicity. And yet, constantly bent forward in an attempt to breathe, but also shrinking into itself through exhaustion, the Captain's eroded face seemed like the desperate face of a deep-water denizen raised from a shipwrecked grave. Was this the physical manifestation of my current path? I too was a captain, albeit with less years of experience, but with the ambition to make up the difference. I was on leave to visit Ms. Palatine during this month in some far off country. She'd been convinced that the Captain would, "inform my view of the profession. You'll love him. You will."

However, to my eye, the Captain possessed the distinct pallor of flotsam; pieces of him seemed to float disconnected on the surface of some distant sea. He hadn't spoken, beyond a grunt of introduction, since Ms. Palatine had brought him into the room. I wondered if he was indeed endowed with speech. Ms. Palatine was gesticulating wildly in an attempt to convey the movements of a man-of-war she'd once seen off the coast of Portugal when the Captain brutally interceded.

"You're a woman," he said to me like he'd made a discovery. I couldn't deny it.

Without allowing space for rebuttal, he continued. "Have you been to the Timor Islands?"

I hadn't, and in fact had never heard of them.

"That's what did this to me," he said in a grumble of pain. "The bulk of my thought, I left it there. My reproductive instinct no longer stirs because I created an existence for the greater part of my thoughts, and I left them on the islands to live on without me. Now I lead the vegetative life of a convalescent." His eyes, whose azure luminescence I only now discovered, shone vaguely dazed like the eyes, indeed, of a man whose life drifted far from here.

I could hear the beating of a very small heart somewhere equally far away.

"Isn't that nice," Ms. Palatine thrust her voice into the antiquated moment. "You've bought an island! Good for you, Captain!"

"Madam," the Captain said, "I did not buy an island. I left my life on one to outlive me."

"To outlive you! Imagine that. Have you ever heard of such a thing?"

I didn't respond to Ms. Palatine's comment, but she was correct; the Captain had informed my view of my profession. In fact, with these few words, it would be more correct to say that he'd significantly altered my view, but in what way, I was not yet sure. With the Captain's words, I arrived in a liminal space. Something had shifted, and would continue to shift.

His eyes drifted off somewhere else. I had no urge to follow.

~

The next time I saw the Captain I did so from above. He lay in Ms. Palatine's attic bedroom. I'd come to pay my respects to the man who cut me from my tethers. The Captain seemed to be singing those present a long, happy song that filled the room with a buoyant light. I soon realized the song was an unconscious hoarse rattle coming from his mouth. It must have been induced by the morphine, which allowed the Captain's breathing to no longer labor, but rise quick and musical. It fluttered deliquescent. The long phrase that issued from his bearded mouth rose higher and higher, dancing in swooping arabesques before dissolving somewhere near the ceiling.

Ms. Palatine, so gesticulative and effusive before, had grown appropriately somber for the bedside. Others had been notified and were supposedly soon to arrive. Who they were I did not know, and in fact of the dozen darkly clad people crammed into the room, I knew none besides Ms. Palatine. They all seemed to be old sea-faring men, half whale, half man. I imagined I saw a dorsal fin. None of them spoke. The air in the room held a strange suffusion of body odor, the scent of life, and the stench of death. I wouldn't have been surprised if some of the death wafted out of a few of the gathered men, for whom it seemed their own deathbed vigil might soon begin. I'd already been in the room for two hours and the thought of more bodies crammed into the already suffocatingly hot room was beyond what I considered my duty. And so I said my goodbyes to Ms. Palatine and departed.

Ms. Palatine contacted me the next day. They needed a boat on which to take the Captain's body for a burial at sea. Someone had suggested my boat, because I was absent from the sea's economy. What could I say? I agreed, and later that day my boat was full of the same darkly clad people from the bedside. Ms. Palatine, with a certain gleam of pride in her eye, said she'd stayed another nine hours after I left at the Captain's bedside. There were only a few of us left at the end. The faithful. The Captain's eyes flew open strangely peaceful as if to take one last look at the world's belongings before parting, one last life-gulp, then the breathing stopped. The living mourn by carrying their grief towards a light. Is the light a sun? Upon a sea? The Captain, even in his departing, seemed to take a clear view of such necessity.

~

The Captain, in his dress uniform, lies on a wooden raft, his body soaked in gasoline. The archers release and push the raft from my boat. It is a clear evening, the gloaming, the light with a palliative quality in which we are suspended. Soon the colors of the sky will be gone. The raft drifts. When it is nearly forty yards away, the archers, the same old men from the bedside whom I supposed were so near death, light their arrow tips. Their arms move with surprising fluidity. They take aim together, bows taught, quivering, a flame at the end of their arms. Ms. Palatine, standing with a firm presence in front of the gathered, utters a few words as prayer in a guttural language I am far from comprehending, and the arrows fly.

In the shadows that flash over him as he makes his

way from wave to wave, I glimpse the immensity of the mechanism in which I am caught, the utter fragility of my own flotilla, composed as it is of these ceaselessly passing shadows, night to day to night, carried forward by the very motion that devours me: my asking. And then the Captain's body is lit.

We watch the flames. "What was his name?" I ask Ms. Palatine, "all this time and I never knew his name." Without looking in my direction, eyes fixed on the pyre, she says, "Marcel. His name was Marcel." I nod. It seems familiar to me, but why I can't say. "He was also quite an accomplished author," Ms. Palatine adds, "though I've never read his work. It's said to be quite...long. Wordy. Page-long sentences, pages without a paragraph break. A friend once described it as an incomprehensibly long amount of time to spend in bed. Too long if you ask me, but I did enjoy his company." "I never knew," I respond. The wind changes. "The things we don't know..."

THE ARC OF THE EVERLASTING:
A SINGLE DREAM

I am about to tell you an account of a year of my life, a wasted year in which I thought I'd accomplish so much, but instead accomplished nothing. Or almost nothing, and what I did manage to accomplish, the one thing during the entire year, I cannot take credit for. An entire year set aside to work, and what do I get out of it? A single dream.

Barbara Robichaux was the caretaker of the largest cemetery in the county and she lived in the modest caretaker's cabin near the entrance. As we rode in her golf cart the three miles back into the heart of Reclamation Yard, Barbara said, "of course, come winter, this road'll be completely snowed in, no access whatsoever. You'll have to snowshoe out, or ski, if you want."

As we drove and the little electric motor whined at full force, I leaned back to watch the leaves stream by, accumulating into rustic blur, a painterly swath of abstraction that reminded me, for some reason, of alchemy, a subject I knew absolutely nothing about, but I noticed in this association, a desperate desire for transformation.

The hut I would live in for the next nine months lacked electricity, heated by a fat but slender wood stove, a pile of wood blanketed along an outside wall.

As Barbara prepared to drive the golf cart back to the entrance of Reclamation Yard, I reassessed the now seemingly paltry pile of wood. "Do you think that'll last me the whole winter?" I called out. Barbara braked, turning her tangle of red hair back in my direction and with the smoker's grackle in her voice that would so haunt me in the future, said, "I have no idea, Mr. Auden—what do you think I am, a woodchuck?" I had no idea what this last reference meant, but it unsettled me and left me with a sinking feeling like an empty coffer.

When I think of this period of time, so aggrandized, so anticipated for its place and productivity, I think of sludge: a thickly viscous immobile body of blackness whose weight was unfathomable, whose current stagnated and whose density threatened to crush me as an ebony tidal wave looming above a meager soul.

Wooden pews facing the room's center lined three of the interior walls of the hut, presumably left over from some church service, the tall, straight-back variety of pew (is there any other variety?) that allowed absolutely no comfort and forced only the most stiff attention.

In what I came to call the forest cemetery in which my little hut sat, I sometimes observed foxes crunching ever so quietly among the fallen leaves and the low slabs of gravestones, which reminded me of children out for a stroll.

For the entire time I lived in the hut in the midst of Reclamation Yard, I only had one visitor. Even Roberto's visit surprised me, because I had no friends to speak of, never really have had any friends, and certainly didn't expect, indeed even want, anyone to visit. I thought the depth and distance within Resurrection Yard would deter everyone, but not Roberto one late fall morning. I forbade him from talking about school and instead we talked about pop music, or rather Roberto played me some of the latest hits he'd downloaded onto his phone. One's lyrics particularly hung around in my head: "Took a bus to China Town/Standing on Canal/And Bowery/Wishin' you were next to me," then launching into a marchingly catchy chorus about Home. Roberto thought I should throw a party out here at my hut. No one would come, I said. Sure they would, sure they would. Roberto's life was marked by such instances of optimism and generosity. I was glad he'd visited, and I was glad when he left. I never threw the party he suggested, never even considered it. In the momentary space left after Roberto's absence, before the familiar sludge rolled in, I felt a brief lightness.

I could continue to complain about this time of withered libido and even further shrunken inspiration. And it was certainly true that I'd expected so much more from this time that I'd given myself as a gift, that had required me to shift so many other, I'd thought lesser, aspects of my life, all in order to give space for the pure, unadulterated harnessing of my creative fire. Whoa buddy, was I ever wrong about that. The pervasiveness of this depravity is probably best expressed through the following pitiful anecdote. Before I'd begun my year at Reclamation Yard, I decided that to mark the significance of the retreat, I would christen myself with a new name, not a hypocorism, but more of a spirit handle, something that I would call myself to literally summon my creative mystic. I promised myself that I would only use this name during my time there, so that, when I was bustling around the hut making tea, I'd say to myself, "Careful there, Geronimo, don't let that tea steep too long." "Geronimo" was indeed a name I'd initially considered, but then I decided to wait and after a week or so of living at the hut, I'd let the name arise. But of course it never did. I cycled through a plethora of possibilities, hoping for inspiration to stick: Cycleman, Butch, Agave, Titular Rhizome, Hemp Captor, Mr. Vroom-vroom. But no, nothing, none of them.

After what I thought an obscene amount of time without giving myself this new name, I realized it probably would never come, most likely because I hadn't done a lick of creative work beyond choosing what color M&M to eat first. I thus decided, one day, to name myself, regardless of the fact that nothing felt right and I did nothing all day other than read mystery/thriller novels and make elaborate snack plates for myself. My new name: "I hereby christen thee 'Bobo,' Boob of the Cemetery, Bozo of the Lazy, Undone and Undead."

That day was a productive day.

But then I never called myself "Bobo." It felt too

demeaning. Yet it was there, in spirit, hovering around me like a fettered mesh of mosquitoes.

Months and months must've passed. I saw Barbara Robichaux one day. It must've been early spring. She rode by in her golf cart and didn't even stop in to say hello; in fact she didn't even slow the golf cart. Barbara whined by, head held high, talking on her cell phone. I watched her go by like I was watching a chance glimpse of Santa and his sleigh. She waved like a neighbor, and as she waved, she called out: "I'ma talkin' to my Sweat Art!" I found myself desperate to talk to her, talk at her, bombard her with my petty thoughts, and let her quotidian concerns wash over me. But she disappeared before this train of thought finished. Oh Bobo, you are a real boob, a real bozo.

It must've been that night. That had to have been the fateful night during which something actual worthwhile happened. But as I mentioned, I couldn't take credit for it; it was a dream.

A hand held a metal spoon that poured three different colored (left-yellow; middle-blue; right-red) warm washes over my penis. I enjoyed all three of them, at first, then I realized the point of the act was for me to choose one. I also intuited that the washes differed in thickness, and thus too in intensity, and so I chose red, as it was the most intense, though I don't know now why I particularly valued its intensity, which, in waking reflection, seemed minutely different from the other two colors.

Then it became clear that the point of the dream was to open my third eye. As soon as this realization came to me, I found myself inexplicably on a large sailboat, spread out on the stern, fornicating with Barbara Robichaux. Ah, how I struggled with what word to use in that last sentence: 'fucking', 'having sex', 'copulating', 'boning'? Nothing felt right, and in fact, there may not be a word for the type of act in which we were engaged. Regardless of the verb, I was more that a little disturbed, and even in the dream it felt like enforced sex, yet it continued to happen. And for my part, I did nothing to stop it. I could tell Barbara was working, as if she were the spiritual advisor with whom the responsibility of my third eye lay. That's not to say she wasn't enjoying herself. At one moment in the act, I began to stop, as the whole thing just felt too bizarre, but Barbara yelled out, "What do you think you're doing? Keep going!" She lay back on the varnished wood of the hull and moaned. Then I woke up.

The last time I saw Barbara Robichaux was the day I left the hut at the back of Reclamation Yard. She was fiddling with something in the dinky engine of her beloved golf cart, which had apparently ceased running. I told her I was leaving the hut early, neglecting to mention my reason for leaving. Is that so, she said, straightening up from the golf cart, running a hand through her hair, which I now noticed contained much more gray than I'd previously noticed. Suit yourself. Barbara looked me up and down, a withering pass-over

I usually associated with truck stop diners appraising an approaching waitress. She paused at my head, steadying her gaze in the middle of my forehead. An uncomfortable moment passed with her eyes silently upon me. Well, she finally said, I'm glad it all worked out for you. I mumbled meekly in the affirmative, my face reddening uncontrollably. I'm glad you got what you came for.

Journey of the Swim, or
Cannery: A Parable of Reproduction

May we be blessed by
the spirits of these fish
    — from (sardine factory, Belfast)
      by Gary Lawless

S uch things only happen in the summer up here. They'd closed it up for good some time ago. But that just opened it for a different kind of commerce. He was up from down south, kept making his way north, farther and farther, a drifter, a musician who went by the name of Brother Adam, but who wasn't really a musician, only told people that, more of a drifter with a harmonica to fit the image.

With a snap, a pry and a squeeze, he was in. Stale air layered above the forever linger of fish. He didn't mind. Never did, you go on and live with it. Tell you one thing, he ain't gonna change much. He settled in. As much as ever. The air seemed to pass through his hollowed mind, not an easy feat, but he'd done it through roads and time. He hid it all in his big, bushy white beard, and after enough years, beard absorbed it, took him in and left him there with pleasant eyes of a pale shade.

He moved around. This took a few weeks. His portly form, recognized around town, got called "Gandalf" a few times by some punk kids, fine, let them laugh, "Fat

Gandalf." Indeed, harrumph. Whatever.

He came home at night, careful not to shine lights too obvious in the fishery windows. Took to eating sardines with fingers, in honor of his surroundings, an offering to the fishery gods of past, bit of a sacrifice at first, then he grew to like them. And of course, those little fishies cheap, yeah. Got them at the dollar store where everything except sardines is more than a dollar, seventy-five cents, as they should be. Used to say, we were packed liked sardines, i.e. small, cheap, tightly-packed. He was not a sardine in the cannery, no, one measly fat gray sardine in a large hollow tin, dark and full of echoes.

One night, he heard a noise among the noises, a singular clank among the many tiny mouse/rat jangles. Ignore it, must be nothing, making it up, hearing things. Imagining. Stars. Make that sound. He sang to himself and it went away. Didn't hear it again. Only the dripping of time.

He went back out and out into the days of the week as he'd always done, against the onslaught of the wonderful story that wasn't, against death and everybody, and the perpetual unanswerable question: where you from? Something was always lost.

He muttered this to himself, smiled, ducked and pried his way into the cannery, downed the light, and walked as if through the salt cod black sea—

A falling shoosh and suddenly he was surrounded by something like shantung, first word that came to his mind, don't know why, but whatever the fabric, it draped on him with a stultifying gauze weight, couldn't move and when he tried, he only made it worse.

He bellowed.

"You sound like a sea cow. Relax." A woman's voice. She stepped out. "I caught ya, didn't I? Netted ya just like they used to in the old days out there on the high seas."

He grunted.

"Didn't I, didn't I..." She tittered and paced, did a little gotcha-shuffle and her rag of robes spun around her in a twirling fanfare. "Yes I did."

The hours revealed her to be Anty, or maybe Aunty, she didn't spell it. Another drifter, but with a bit of a... weird streak. He didn't know. She had as much gray hair on her head as he did on his face; together, they'd be a full head face ball of gray.

"You're such a catch," she said like he was a young doctor who she'd lassoed into marriage.

After some time, his blood pressure came back down, he could think again, talk.

"Water..." he croaked. "Water..."

"Oh you big baby, I'm not going to starve you. I ain't gonna let you waste away."

And she didn't. She fed him nice. Hot coffee from somewhere, tasty little victuals for the setting, chips, cured meat. But she also didn't let him go. She stayed chatty. In time everything changes, and although they were still strangers with an element of danger, they became something else.

Anty told him her story, the glossed-over version that hid the deep and terrible lows—they weren't that close yet—but spun them into an honest, vulnerable pitch with a pinch of sass.

Brother Adam began to talk too beneath the net. It was like he was talking through a darkened web, because he was, but for some reason, surprising to him, this was comforting, and indeed even inspired a certain loquacity that hadn't peeked out of him in years and years of downtrodden. Captivity, in fact, seemed to suite him, giving way to a cannery domesticity that eventually forced them to confront each other.

"What are we doing?!"

"Why did you trap me?"

"Why didn't you put up more of a fight?"

"Are you crazy?"

"Are you crazy?"

Indeed, love, or one of its derivatives, had taken root. And speaking of root, she got under the net there with him. In other words, they fucked like old people, which is to say they knew what they were doing, which is to say they also didn't want to hurt themselves. The cannery took on another fishy smell. They complimented each other.

Time passed in little crunk components. Little fits and starts. Dissolved, bubbled back up to float, pool, eddy, rage forward with a king tide, and pull way back to the ocean's edge.

Spring came and they didn't hate each other. Then, strangest of strangest, she began to show.

"What's that?"

"My bump."

"Your bump. You bump like that? You been swallowing whole bowling balls?"

"I think I'm bumping a baby."

"Thought you mega-paused and all that."

"Me too. Guess not."

"Huh. Don't know what I think about that."

"Me neither."

And so they did their best not to think about it at all. But, as babies do, that belly interjected itself into about everything. It had its way. Emergent. Like everybody's already been born and I want to do it too.

"Will I have a gray-haired baby?" she thought, "an old soul? As they say…" She prepared. She didn't know who "they" were, but knew they did indeed talk.

He thought about the old days, thought back as far as he could, but couldn't get back to babydom, that misty memory field fallow as any blackness. What would they do?

The problem was that time ate itself, and before either of them had a bead on perpetuity, it came out in a rush of water. The baby. The boy. A whole lot of loving to keep my baby happy, true true, and they called him Sardine, because of his silvery skin, puckered mouth and he was so darn small, compact. How it takes a whole lot of kissing and hugging. A whole lot of decision-making.

And they decided, or it was decided for them because the weather was getting warmer, earlier, and it became harder to be themselves with their squatting frugality in a swelling town of tourists, and so they decided to set their baby free, because all babies, as everybody knows, want to be free and so they set Sardine into the ocean to be free, feed everybody with his flesh, ubiquitous, breed and make merry. Throw your young body against the waves and come up clean, son, once uncountable volumes, come back, quicksilver, come back, torn by the spirits swimming through our world. In a word: hope.

I would like to thank the people who helped bring this book into the world: Heather & Tod for connection and synchronicity, Alina Gallo for her cover painting, Kathy Hooke for her insightful editorial eye, and Maria Northcott & Joyce Sampson for their photographs. For the teachers and friends who have nurtured my writing: Megan Grumbling, Sarah Heller, Emily Skyrm, John Miller, Paul Bennett, Bhanu Kapil, Reed Bye, Laird Hunt, Mike Bove, David Stankiewicz, Howard Rosenfield & Playwrights Circle, and Kevin Sweeney. And to the following people and places that have inspired me and some of these stories: Kimberly & Anthony Eames & family, Kyle, Ross Bennett, Isa, Jed, & Nils Rathband and Kenna Ferguson, Robert Vettese, Chris Hoffmann, Denis Nye, Gary Lawless, Stephen Petroff, Colin Sullivan-Stevens, Rob Lieber, Susan Gallo, Gordon Bok, Sarah Orne Jewett, Douglas Alvord, Paul Auster, Bernadette Mayer, Shirley Hazzard, Earle Shettleworth, Proust, Nathaniel Hawthorne, Aurora Provisions, AAA, Red's in Wiscasset, Waldorf schools, St. Luke's Cathedral, The Captain Lindsey House, South Freeport, Sacred & Profane, The Maine Arts Commission, Route 1, Belfast, The Maine Historical Society, *The First Line*, The Portland Museum of Art, and Peaks Island. Most importantly, I would like to thank my family, especially my parents for the important nudge that got me on the plane to Boulder, and Sarah for all your love and ideas, including the title of this book (even if you don't remember coming up with it).

Joyce Sampson

JEFFERSON NAVICKY was born in Chicago and grew up in Southeastern Ohio. He earned a B.A. from Denison University and an M.F.A. from Naropa University. He is the author of *The Book of Transparencies* (KERNPUNKT Press) and the chapbooks *Uses of a Library* (Ravenna Press) and *Map of the Second Person* (Black Lodge Press). His work has been published in Smokelong Quarterly, apt, Hobart, Tarpaulin Sky, and Fairy Tale Review. He is the archivist at the Maine Women Writers Collection and teaches English at Southern Maine Community College. Jefferson lives in Freeport, Maine.

Made in the USA
Middletown, DE
28 November 2018